BULLETS OF REVENGE

BULLETS OF REVENGE

RAYMOND PICK

Matador
5 Weir Road
Kibworth Beauchamp
Leicester LE8 0LQ, UK
Tel: (+44) 116 279 2299
Fax: (+44) 116 279 2277
Email: books@troubador.co.uk
Web: www.troubador.co.uk/matador

ISBN 978 1848764 255

British Library Cataloguing in Publication Data.
A catalogue record for this book is available from the British Library.

Typeset in 11pt Sabon MT by Troubador Publishing Ltd, Leicester, UK

Matador is an imprint of Troubador Publishing Ltd

Printed in Great Britain by the MPG Books Group, Bodmin and King's Lynn

To my mother, I owe you everything

A SOLDIER

A soldier's duty is to defend his country and to fight *for* a just cause. If the reasons for going into battle are all lies, he should refuse to fight or desert. No man should die for the lies of a politician.

Raymond Pick

PARIS

He took another sip of his cognac. It was a warm August evening, and at last he was beginning to relax as he sat in a café on the Boulevard Saint-Germain. The investigation into the murder of a young prostitute was over, and Anderson, a middle-aged cab driver, was going on trial. As he finished his drink, an attractive brunette sat down at a nearby table. After a while, he noticed that she was watching him. As he looked at her, she gave him a friendly smile. He wasn't a shy man, so he walked up to her table and said in French, "May I sit down and join you?"

"Yes," she said, "why not?"

"Let me introduce myself. My name is James Ransome. And you are?"

"Adele Foulard."

A waiter came up to the table and asked, "Would you like something to drink?"

"Some red wine, please. And I'll have a whisky."

After the waiter left, Adele said, "You speak very good French."

He smiled. "Yes, my mother made sure of that. She was French. What do you do for a living, Adele?"

"I'm a secretary. And you?"
"I'm a detective."
"So what are you doing in Paris, chasing criminals?"
"No, just relaxing. I needed a break."
He found her very warm and friendly. They had some more drinks and sat there talking for hours. He took her home, and they arranged to see a show the next day. Four months later they were married in a large church ceremony with a hundred guests. Their honeymoon was on the Greek island of Ithaca. They bought a house in Barnet and settled down to married life.
One day, Adele looked at her husband and asked, "Any regrets?"
"No, I knew you were the one the first time I saw you."

A year later he took his wife to the hospital where they had their first child, a boy. He was christened John William Ransome, and nine months later, their daughter Jennifer was born. One weekend shortly after his son's twelfth birthday, he was in the kitchen making coffee when Adele walked in.
"Do you want a coffee?"
"Yes, please."
They took their coffees into the lounge and sat down.
"You know, Adele, our kids seem to be doing alright at school, but every school has its bad apples, and I don't want them to be bullied or influenced by the bad kids. They need to know how to handle themselves, so I want them to learn karate. It will make them more disciplined and confident to deal with any trouble that comes their

way. I will make sure they persevere and make a success of it. I'm going to call them in right now."

James went into the garden and shouted, "John, Jennifer, come into the lounge, I want to talk to you."

They came in and sat down.

"We know we are pretty hard on you sometimes – not allowing you to watch television at weekends, but homework is more important, and television is for zombies anyway. We don't allow you to eat junk food because we don't want fat kids. Now I want to talk about school. In every school there are good kids and bad kids. I never want you to do what the bad kids do. Always use your judgment; if it's not a good thing, don't do it. Do not become bullies because they only end up being hated. Do not follow kids who take drugs; taking drugs isn't cool, isn't smart and will just mess up your life. Always be strong; drugs are for the weak and the stupid. Always remember we love you both very much, and if you have any problems, come to us and we will sort them out."

KARATE

The following week, John and Jennifer were at the dojo taking their first lesson. They went twice a week and both enjoyed the lessons. They were taught the Shotokan style, and after a few weeks, Ransome wanted to know where the style originated from and decided to find out.

The Shotokan style of karate was developed by Gechin Funakoshi (1868–1957). He was born in Okinawa as a premature baby and raised by his maternal grandmother. He suffered from poor health, and in the hope of improving it, his grandmother sent him to train with a karate master called Azato. His health did get better, and in 1888 he passed his exams and became a teacher. He continued his training and saw his karate master every night. In 1921 the Crown Prince of Japan visited Okinawa and saw one of Funakoshi's demonstrations. He was very impressed and invited Funakoshi to perform at the first National Athletic Exhibition in 1922. He was asked to stay in Japan and give more demonstrations of his art, which he did, and Shotokan karate became very popular, with many clubs being opened for its instruction. Later, it would spread to the rest of the world.

At John and Jennifer's dojo, their training was divided into three parts. They learnt the basics (kihon) as beginners, and later, kata, which is a sequence of moves against imaginary opponents consisting of kicks, sweeps, punches, throws, blocks and strikes. After that, it was kumite, sparring against real opponents. Their sensei was a Fifth Dan, who believed in hard training and strict discipline, but he was a good teacher.

One year later, they moved house and changed school. On the first day, during a lesson, the class bully threw a small empty plastic drink bottle at Ransome, followed by a plastic cup. Ransome turned round and looked at him, the bully and his cronies just smiled. After the lesson finished, Ransome was first to leave the classroom. He waited until the bully walked into the corridor and then punched him in the jaw. He fell on the floor, and as he lay there, Ransome said, "You throw things at me again, you'll get a lot more than a punch in the jaw."

HELPING JENNIFER

After that incident, Ransome wasn't bothered by the bully or anyone else. He had been doing karate for two years and had gained a lot of confidence in fighting. One Saturday evening he went to a party with his sister, and while Jennifer gossiped with her friends, he talked about football with the boys.

Later, Jennifer needed to use the bathroom. As she was looking for it, a drunken youth tried to pull her into one of the bedrooms.

"Let go of me, you drunken pig!" Jennifer yelled, kicking and punching him.

Just then, Ransome appeared. He had left the party to get some fresh air and saw what was happening. He went up to the youth and hit him in the face, breaking his nose, and the blood squirted out; then he dragged him into the bathroom and left him there.

He returned to his sister and said, "Come on, let's go. The party isn't any good anyway."

As they were walking home, Jennifer said, "You know, John, you're getting to be quite a tough guy."

"I don't know about that, but nobody picks on you and gets away with it."

After the incident at the party, James Ransome had a word with his young son.

"John, you are getting to be a violent individual."

"Well, Dad, on the first day during a lesson the class bully threw an empty plastic bottle and paper cup at me. I wasn't going to stand for that. At the party, a drunk was trying to pull Jennifer into one of the bedrooms; she was fighting him, and I thought I would give her a hand."

"Look here, John, I'm in the police. I can't have my son getting involved in violence, so just cool it down a bit."

Later that night, he and his wife Adele were lying in bed talking about their son.

"Did you have a word with John?" Adele asked.

"Yes, the boy at school was a bully and needed to be taught a lesson; the drunk trying to drag Jennifer into a bedroom deserved what he got. I couldn't really tell him off. The bad guys in this world need to be knocked down, I don't want our son to be a weakling; it's a hard world."

Adele was quiet for a minute, and then said, "Apart from being a karate fanatic, he has a remarkable interest in foreign languages. I just wonder how he will turn out. He is fourteen now and getting excellent grades. If he carries on studying, he can go to university and be anything he wants to be – a doctor or a lawyer."

"Adele, I think you are way off the mark. He has an appetite for danger. I can't see him sitting on his bum all day, working in an office. I've asked him what he wants to do when he's older, and he said he intends to get his A-levels. After that, he wants to travel and spend a year or two abroad. He is saving his money now and should have enough by the time he is eighteen, and if it runs out on one of his trips he will do odd jobs to pay his way. Then he's going to join the Royal Marines or the French Foreign Legion."

Adele began to cry. He kissed her and asked, "What's the matter, darling, why the tears?"

"I had hoped he would go to university and then get a good job, marry a nice girl and settle down; instead, he wants to go round the world and join the army."

"Adele, you have to accept that he has an adventurous spirit. He trains hard and studies hard; he's a good kid. We cannot run his life. At least he's not one of those pathetic drug addicts trapped in the slime of drug abuse."

They carried on talking for another half an hour and then went to sleep.

When he was sixteen, Ransome got his black belt in Shotokan Karate. At eighteen, he had to make a decision about his future. He had passed five A-levels: English, Spanish, French, German and Japanese, and was pleased with the results. He liked the thought of visiting different countries and speaking their language, whilst the prospect of going to university did not excite him at all. He decided to spend a year in Japan, training and improving his knowledge of karate. In his spare time, he would give private English lessons to help finance his stay.

JAPAN

The day before his departure to Japan, Adele had prepared an evening meal. As they were finishing it off with walnut cake and coffee, she asked, "John, do you have to go for a year? It's a long time, and I'm going to miss you a lot."

"You know me, Mother; I have to be doing things, not sitting around watching TV or working in a boring job."

She gave a sad smile and said, "Yes, I know I have an adventurer for a son." Jennifer touched his arm, saying, "After you've been there four or five months, I would like to come over for a week or two and see the sights."

"Yes, okay."

His father looked at him. "You've done well with your exams and I'm very pleased. I've got something for you." He took £1,000 out of his pocket and gave it to him. "A little expenses money for your trip."

"Thanks, Dad, it will come in very handy."

The next day, he said goodbye to his parents and sister, and took the plane to Japan. The flight was eleven hours. From the airport, he went by the Narita Express to Shinjuku Station, the busiest station in the world. He changed some money and bought a ticket from one of the machines, and got on the train for a fifteen-minute journey to his hostel. Once there, he unpacked and went to bed.

The next morning at breakfast, he reviewed his plans. He was going to relax for the next three weeks, sightseeing in Tokyo and other places outside the capital. Then, he would look for a dojo to improve his karate and do some English teaching to earn some money.

After he finished his breakfast, he went out into the noisy, crowded streets. First, he went to the Tokyo Tower in Shiba Park. It was taller than the Eiffel Tower; from its highest point, all of Tokyo is visible, and on a clear day Mount Fuji can be seen. Next on the agenda was the Tokyo National Museum. It opened in 1872 and was the first museum in Japan. The museum holds over 110,000 objects and five galleries, and has the largest collection of Japanese art in the world, including paintings, textiles, national treasures and lacquerware. He spent the whole day there.

Over the next few days, he visited three more museums, including the Sword Museum. He had a quiet side and was fascinated by all that he had seen.

On the fourth day, he was up early and having breakfast in the hostel when two young men entered, looked around the dining room and approached his table. One was about six-feet tall, the other was a bit shorter. They were both well built and wore casual clothes. The taller one spoke first and stuck out his hand.

"Hi, I'm Floyd Canton, from New York."

Ransome shook his hand. "John Ransome, London."

Then the other man shook his hand and said, "Dave Appleby, also from New York."

He invited them to sit down and asked, "Why don't you guys order some breakfast?"

As they were eating, he asked Floyd, "So, what are you guys doing in Tokyo?"

"It's the last country on our Asian tour. We've been to China, India, Hong Kong, Malaysia and Thailand. After we get back to the States, we're going to join the US Army." He continued, "And you, what brings you to Japan?"

"I want to improve my karate and practise my Japanese, but I'm doing some sightseeing first."

"You speak Japanese?"

"Yeah."

"Say, John, why don't we visit some places together?"

"Yeah, that's a good idea."

They went to Kyoto, Hiroshima and Yokohama, and climbed Mount Fuji. Ransome was sorry when the time came for his friends to leave. On the last night, they went to a Japanese restaurant and had a good meal and plenty to drink. They promised to keep in touch.

After Ransome had been in Tokyo for five months, his sister came for a holiday. He went to Narita Airport to meet her, and after she had passed through customs they greeted and hugged each other.

"It's been a long time."

"Jennifer, I've only been away five months."

"It seems longer than that."

"How are Mum and Dad?"

"Mum complains that you don't write home enough. She misses you badly."

"I'll ring her tonight. Now, let's get a taxi. You can stay at my place."

On the way, he asked, "What are you doing now?"

"Media studies – I like it, it's pretty interesting."

Over the next two weeks, he took her to the most interesting sights. It was a completely new world for her, as she had only been to Europe before. He introduced her to all his friends. She was young and beautiful and they tried to chat her up, but she was having none of it.

After her holiday was over, he went back to his training and teaching English. The months flew by and soon his year was over. His karate had greatly improved and he spoke Japanese fluently. He phoned home and told them that he was returning.

Adele heard the front door being unlocked and rushed over; she kissed and hugged him. "John, it's so good to have you home again."

"It's good to be back, Mum."

His father and Jennifer heard his voice in the hallway and came over to greet him.

"Come into the lounge, John, and let's all have a drink to celebrate your return."

As they were having dinner, his father asked, "What do you plan to do now, John?"

"I want to stay in London for a while to earn some money so that I can go abroad again, but this time I won't be away so long."

Nine days later, he started work as a salesman. His

parents didn't ask him for any money, so in five months, when he thought he had saved enough, he left work and went to America. He visited New York, Las Vegas, Los Angeles, Miami, San Francisco, saw the Grand Canyon and Niagara Falls, and then went to Washington DC. After he had seen all he wanted, he returned home.

THE LEGION

Ransome had always wanted to join the army. He considered the Royal Marines or the Parachute Regiment; the British Army was one option, another was the French Foreign Legion. He could never quite shake off the attraction of the Legion, there was always something mysterious and romantic about it. Its recruits were a mixture of adventurers, ex-soldiers, petty criminals and unemployed men; some wanted to hide their past and establish a new identity, whilst others could simply not settle down to a normal civilian life. In the end, he chose the Legion.

The next day he took the train to Paris. He arrived at the Gare du Nord, bought a drink and a ham baguette, and sat down at one of the tables. It was good to be in Paris again. He spent a couple of days relaxing, and on the third day he went to the recruitment centre at Fort du Nogent and banged on the huge doors. He told the Legionnaire who opened them that he wanted to join the Legion. Ransome was led into an office, behind the desk sat a smart-looking corporal.

"I wish to join the Legion," Ransome said in French.

"Why?"

"Because it's one of the best forces in the world."

"Passport."

He put it down on the desk, and the corporal proceeded to ask him several questions. "You speak very good French?"

"Yes, I've always liked the language."

"Are you sure you want to join? Five years is a long time, and the training is hard; it has to be."

"Yes, I want to join."

He was taken into a hall where there were about thirty men sitting on benches. He looked around and listened – there were at least five different languages being spoken. He went up to a small group who were speaking in English and spoke to one of them.

"It's nice to know I'm not the only Englishman here."

"Yeah, we're outnumbered. My name is Pete Johnson. Yours?"

"John Ransome."

Johnson was of medium build with short hair and brown eyes. He introduced him to the others.

"Next to you is Vic Thomas; the other two are Roger Masters and Alan Eastman. Vic and I are ex-paratroopers, Roger was in the Marines and Alan is ex-SAS."

"What made you want to join the Legion?" Pete asked.

"I had read about it, and it seemed to be so different from anything else. I always wanted to be a soldier," Ransome responded. "And you?"

"After leaving the paratroopers I tried life as a civilian for a year, but I got bored stiff. I thought I would give this lot a try."

Vic and Roger also said they were bored. Alan gave another reason.

"After leaving the SAS," he said, "I met this blond and had an affair. It proved to be very dangerous, and I had to leave London in a hurry; maybe one day I will tell you the story."

The next day, all the recruits had to sign their contracts for a six-month probationary period, during which the contract could be terminated by the Legion if it thought the recruit did not meet its standards. After they had signed these, they went to have their hair cut and receive their uniforms. When they were back in their barracks room, Ransome spoke to Alan. "You know, I'm not happy about having my hair shaved off."

"Don't worry; we won't be going out chasing girls." They both laughed.

The room was full of cigarette smoke, and his new friends played poker until the lights went out.

The next morning they were woken by the sound of a bugle. After a wash and a shave, they went down to breakfast of coffee, and half a baguette and jam; it wasn't much and they were all still hungry. The Legion does not employ civilians; the Legionnaires do the cleaning. Ransome was sent to the kitchen while Roger ended up cleaning the toilets. Three days later, they left Fort du Nogent and boarded a train for Marseilles.

FIGHT

As the train sped through the French countryside, Vic asked, “Where are we going, John?”

“First to Marseilles; there, we change trains and go to Aubagne, the Legion’s headquarters.”

They arrived in Aubagne early in the morning. At the camp, any luggage they had was examined and taken away for storage; afterwards, they had a shower and were given their uniforms. Later, there was a lecture in French about the Legion, from its origins dating back to 1831 to the present day. At that time, there were many refugees and deserters from foreign armies in Paris and other parts of France, and King Louis-Philippe felt that they added to the country’s political turmoil. Therefore, on 10 March 1831 he created the French Foreign Legion, the plan was for the men to enlist in the Legion and then be sent to the French colonies for service. The Legion has fought in many countries since its formation, and one of its most famous battles was in a village called Camerone in Mexico. Since most recruits don’t speak French, they have to ask for translations from those who do, but as time passes, and with the aid of French lessons, their knowledge improves and they all end up acquiring the language.

Later that evening, Ransome and his friends sat on their bunks talking.

"How long do you think we will be here, John?"

"About three weeks, until the Legion decides who will be accepted for basic training at Castelnaudary."

The next morning they went for medical examinations; they all passed. The Legion has a security section that questions all recruits, and Ransome had to answer several questions about his background. Having got through that successfully, he was told he could change his name if he wanted to and be given a new identity. The IQ tests were next. In the examination room, an English-speaking corporal addressed them.

"Answer the questions carefully and try to get good marks, as the results you achieve will be used to judge your suitability for any training you may want to take in the future."

In the third week, they were shown around the Legion Museum and saw the famous wooden hand of Captaine Danjou, who was killed in Camerone. They were also given their serial numbers and the famous white hat, the Kepi Blanc, and were accepted for basic training. They were in good spirits as they boarded the train with other recruits for the four-hour journey to Castelnaudary. In the barracks room, there was a big, strong German called Dieter Fleischer who, for some reason, had taken a dislike to Ransome, and whenever Ransome entered the room Fleischer would shout an insult at him. Ransome was going to teach him a lesson, but he didn't want to do it when the corporal was present; his opportunity came that evening.

When he entered the room, Fleischer shouted, "Hey, Ransome, how come your mother let you out of the house? The Legion is not going to make a man out of a wimp like you."

Ransome looked at him and said in a cold voice, "You are a stupid pig, and time will show no improvement."

His face red with fury, Fleischer leapt up and attacked Ransome with a punch aimed at his head. Ransome sidestepped and kicked him in the face, following up with an inside sweep to his leg that unbalanced him, and he landed on the floor. As he tried to get up, Ransome kicked him in the face again.

Alan, who had watched the fight, said, "That was very neat, John. We all wondered how long you were going to put up with his taunts."

"Yeah, I just wanted to make sure the corporal wasn't around when I dealt with him." Fleischer eventually regained consciousness and slowly got to his feet.

On the next inspection, Corporal Durant noticed the state of Fleischer's face and asked, "What happened to you?"

"I fell over."

Durant hit him in the stomach. "Don't lie to me, Fleischer." At that time in the Legion, sergeants and corporals were often violent to recruits who did not do things to their satisfaction or made them angry in some way.

During one of the breaks, Ransome asked Alan, "I'm curious; why did you have to leave London in a hurry?"

COULD NOT RESIST HER

"Listen, John, I'm going to tell you the story, but don't tell anyone else. I was on my fifth scotch in a pub in the East End, when a tall well-dressed mean-looking guy came in. He was accompanied by a young blonde and two other guys who looked like bodyguards. They got their drinks and sat down. About ten minutes later, another guy walked in and spoke to the guy with the blonde, who began to look very angry. He got up and said to her. 'Hey, let's go.' 'But, Billy we've only just got here, I want to stay and finish my drink and have another one.' 'Okay, stay, but not too long, and get back to the flat.' The four of them left, and the blonde stayed behind. She was sitting opposite me, sipping her drink. She was beautiful, about twenty, with long blonde hair. Her lipstick was a nice shade of red, she had a slim figure and wore a tight white blouse, black trousers and black high-heeled shoes – she was about my height. She was gorgeous and she knew it. I had seen the men she had been with and I should have left her alone, but I could not resist her. I went up to her table and sat down. She looked at me and said, 'You must be brave or stupid.' 'Oh yeah, why is that?' I asked.

'Didn't you recognise the guy who was with me?' 'No.' 'It was Billy Mays,' 'The London Gangster?' 'Yes, but he prefers to call himself a businessman,' I thought the face had seemed familiar. I had read about him in the papers. He had been arrested and charged with murder, but was later released when the only witness to the crime was shot dead. I should have left at that point, but stayed; maybe it was the drink that was giving me courage. Then she said, 'Now, do you still want to sit here, or have you suddenly discovered you have another appointment?' I said, 'I don't run easy; besides, you're beautiful – I've just got to take you to bed.' She asked me what my name was and said, 'Well, Alan, you've got a lot of nerve; what do you do for a living?' I told her I'd been in the SAS for five years, but had left last week and was wondering what to do next. 'I wouldn't make any plans, Billy is the jealous type; if he finds out you've been trying to chat me up he'll have you beaten up or killed,' she warned me. 'I'll take the chance. What's your name?' I asked. 'Lynne Fairfield.' I asked her how she had met him, and she said, 'I was working as a laptop dancer, and one night Billy was in the club with some of his men sitting at a table drinking champagne. I went up and asked him if he wanted me to dance for him. He said yes, and after a few dances he invited me to his table for some drinks. We started going out together and I became his girlfriend. At the time all I knew was that he was a businessman. It was only later that I found out he was a criminal, but he has always been good to me.' After she had finished talking, she looked at me and said, 'So, you want to take me to bed? Do you think you can satisfy me, make me go the distance? I hope you've got a big one,

Alan, I want more than just a tickle.' 'Sweetheart, I don't think you are going to have any complaints. Lynne, I'm going to tell you my address. Memorise it, don't write it down – the barman has been watching us. Leave about twenty minutes after me. I'm going to get up and leave with a scared expression on my face, and if he asks you anything, tell him that you told me who your boyfriend was and I got very nervous. I'll see you later.' I left the pub and about an hour later there was a knock on my door. I opened it and Lynne stood there with a mischievous glint in her brown eyes. 'Are you going to stand there all day looking at me or are you going to let me in?' I let her in, grabbed hold of her and started to kiss her. We paused for breath, and after a few minutes she said, 'You're a very good kisser, Alan, let's see what you've got down below.' She unzipped my flies and got my knob out, which by now was fully erect. 'Wow, now that's what I call a deadly weapon,' she said. She gave me a blowjob, and after eight or ten minutes I couldn't stand it and shot my load. Then we went into the sixty-nine position. I had her in every way possible, my favourite being doggie style. We saw each other as often as possible and were very careful, but Billy still found out. He never hit her or punished her in any way – he was crazy about her. He saved his hatred for me and tried to have me killed. There were two attempts made on my life, and there would have been more if I hadn't left London. The first was outside my flat. As I got close to my front door, I saw an evil-looking thug standing there. I kicked him in the bollocks just as he was pulling out a knife. He squealed with pain and dropped the knife, then I hit him in the face, and when he was on the ground

I broke his arms. Then I picked him up and threw him on top of a nearby rubbish skip. The next night two men broke into my flat. I beat one with a baseball bat and, in a fight, overpowered the other one. Then I packed my stuff, left the flat and caught the next train to Paris. London was getting too dangerous."

"Was Lynne worth all that trouble?" Ransome asked.

"Yes, before I met her women were just one-night-stands. I wanted to marry her and have some kids, but none of it seems possible now. I hope Billy gets killed by rivals or arrested; then I could take her away. In the meantime, I have a new identity, and after three years I can apply for French citizenship."

Lynne often thought of Alan as time passed. It was a good thing that Billy didn't like children, because she didn't want to have any with him, only with Alan. She knew it was impossible, but she couldn't get the idea out of her mind.

TRAINING

After a week in Castelnaudary they were sent to a farm owned by the Legion for a month's training. This was varied, and included marching, singing, using weapons and learning first aid. Singing is important in the Legion, and all recruits learn to sing in French. To earn the right to wear the Kepi Blanc.

They had to go on a two-day march, and when they got back to camp they were happy they had managed to finish it. At sunset, they were assembled on the parade ground and recited the Legionnaire's Code of Honour in French. On command, they put on the Kepi; it was one of the proudest moments in Ransome's life.

After six weeks, he decided to write home and, as he was doing so, Alan walked in.

"Hello, John. Who are you writing to?"

"Oh, I'm just dropping a line to my parents to let them know how I'm getting on."

"You're lucky, I can't contact home until this problem with Billy is sorted out."

In Castelnaudary there was more weapons training. For Ransome's friends, handling guns was nothing new –

they had all been in the army before – but for him, it was a new experience. He learnt how to use the Famas assault rifle, and fire pistols, machine guns and rifle grenades. He wanted to be an expert, and was determined to stick it out and finish the five years in the Legion; it wouldn't be easy, but life never was. Before their training was over, they were asked to which regiment they wanted to be posted. Ransome and his friends discussed this a short time later.

"Have you decided which regiment you want to be posted to, John?" Alan asked.

"Not yet."

"We're all applying for the 2nd REP, the parachute regiment, although none of us are sure if we'll get the posting; nothing gets the adrenaline going so much as jumping out of a plane."

"Sounds dangerous, count me in."

Their luck was in, and they were informed they were going to Corsica, to Camp Raffalli in Calvi, for their parachute training. They took the ferry from Marseilles for the twelve-hour trip to the island.

Onboard, they put their equipment away and went to look for the bar. Ransome bought the first round. As they were talking, Vic remarked, "You don't drink all that much, John?"

"No, I know my limit. I don't like to get drunk."

Ransome turned in at 11.00 p.m. whilst the others stayed up till late.

When they arrived at camp, a corporal took them to their barracks and said, "You will stay here until your training is finished."

They spent a lot of time in the gym improving their fitness and going on long runs, and then the day finally came for their first jump. Ransome was both excited and apprehensive as he boarded the C160 Transall with the other recruits. Inside the aircraft, the noise of engines made conversation impossible. Soon they reached the drop zone, a side door opened and a red light flashed. The jumpmaster shouted his orders. They got up and hooked themselves up to the overhead metal cable. When the light turned to green, they jumped out. When it was Ransome's turn, he didn't hesitate. He was falling fast; then there was a crack and his parachute opened, slowing down his descent. It was an awesome and fantastic experience to float down in such stillness and silence. He saw Calvi and the others, who had already landed. As the ground neared, he prepared to land and hit the ground hard. Alan, who had landed before him, came up to him.

"How do you feel, John?"

"Absolutely terrific; it was great!"

"It was your first jump, and that's the one you're going to remember most of all."

"Yeah, I'm already looking forward to the next one."

After the parachutes were gathered up, they went to the foyer for drinks.

CALVI

In the summer months, women from all parts of Europe came on holiday to Calvi. Sometimes, Ransome and his friends would go into town for drinks and female company.

Vic was feeling very randy that evening and was determined to get laid. In the first bar they visited, he looked at the women who were there and said, "I don't fancy any of these girls. Come on, let's finish our drinks and go to another place."

The next bar was bigger and noisier. At the end of the bar were six women drinking and talking.

Vic looked at them and said to his friends, "They don't look bad. Let's go over to them and try our luck."

Roger, another member of the group, looked doubtful. "Maybe they don't speak English."

Vic looked at him and smiled. "We'll use sign language."

They went up to the women, and Vic asked the young one he fancied, "Do you speak English?"

"Yes," she said, "where are you from?"

"Paris."

She was in her early twenties and told him her name was Isabelle. She was tall and had black hair and brown eyes, a pretty mouth and a good figure. As she was talking to him, she looked him over and thought he was nice. He had light-brown hair and green eyes, and was nearly as tall as her.

He asked, “Do you have a boyfriend in Paris?”

“I did have, but we broke up. The relationship wasn’t going anywhere. What about you?”

“I had a girlfriend, but we split up when she started using drugs.”

Her English wasn’t bad, and he could see that she liked him. He kissed her, and they had more drinks, laughed, chatted and then they kissed some more.

He asked her, “Can we go up to your room?”

“You don’t waste time, do you, Vic?”

“You’re too beautiful, Isabelle.”

She smiled. “Okay, Englishman, let’s go to my hotel room.”

Going up in the lift, they couldn’t keep their hands off each other and were kissing until they arrived at her floor. When they got to her room, he sat down on the bed and watched her undress. She took off her short red dress and shoes, then her bra and panties. She looked at him and said, “Do you like what you see?”

“Yeah.”

“Come here, we’ll have a shower together.”

He got up and they went into the bathroom. As they were having a shower he groped her, and when they were back in the bedroom they got on the bed and started with some French kissing. He fondled her tits and sucked her nipples, then licked her pussy. Her oral soon had him rock hard, and he put on a condom and gave her a good shafting.

After they had finished, he said, "I want to see you again."

"This is the last day of my holiday. I'm going back to Paris tomorrow; come and see me there when you are on leave. I'll give you my phone number."

"You bet I'm going to see you."

They started kissing again, and then he left and returned to barracks.

The next morning, his friends asked him about the previous night. Vic, who could sometimes be a bit of a loudmouth, said quietly, "We went back to her hotel; the rest I leave to your imagination. I got her phone number and her address, and next time I'm on leave I'm going to see her. I really like her. How did you boys get on with the other girls?" Vic asked.

"We bought them drinks and had a few laughs. They are going back to Paris tomorrow."

"Yeah, I know."

INSIGNIA

After completing another five jumps from a C160 Transall, their parachute training was over. A parade was held, and the colonel awarded them their wings and shook their hands. During their training, they had been asked which company in the 2nd REP they would like to be sent to. As the friends were having a drink after the ceremony, they discussed the relative merits of the six companies. Roger gave his opinion first.

"It's not much good in the CCS. I'm not doing admin or maintenance."

Pete agreed and said, "The CEA looks more interesting. I wouldn't mind using anti-tank missiles or anti-aircraft cannons. What do you think, Vic?"

"I think I like the 1st company, as they fight at night and in the built-up areas."

Pete smiled. "You won't get much sleep, Vic."

Pete looked at Ransome, who said, "The CEA do more than fire heavy weapons; they have some reconnaissance commando units that go behind enemy lines and on special missions. Their training is harder and they do skydiving. To join them, you have to be at least a corporal or of higher rank. I want to see some action, although I'll have to wait for two or three years before I can join them." He turned to Alan and said, "What do you want to do?"

"None of you have mentioned the other companies that do mountaineering and amphibious activities or carry out sabotage, so I guess you're not interested in them. As for me, I'll probably do the same as you, John, and try to get in the reconnaissance unit."

The next day, they were told they were going into the 1st company within a few days, and were sent on an intensive training course – it was very challenging. They were taught how to set booby traps and use dynamite, mines and plastic explosives. They learnt how to cross rivers with ropes, watched live demonstrations of explosives and various unarmed combat techniques were shown. They also practised house-to-house fighting. Ransome knew how to swim, but he had never really messed around with boats, and so using kayaks and inflatable dinghies was something new to him. After they had completed the course, they were awarded their commando insignia.

ON LEAVE

Ransome was feeling good. He was going home on leave and had written to his parents to inform them of the date of his arrival. When Adele read his letter she was overjoyed and prepared for his homecoming. It was raining when he arrived back in London. He made his way home and knocked on the front door. When Adele opened it and saw it was her son, her face lit up with joy.

"Oh, John, it's been so long." She hugged and kissed him and led him into the lounge where his father and sister were sitting.

They got up and embraced him. His father said, "We must all have a drink to welcome you back. What will you have?"

"A large malt, please, Dad."

After they had sat down with their drinks, Adele said, "You're looking very fit, not an ounce of fat."

"Yes, we do a lot of exercise, but they don't overfeed us; in fact, we are always a little hungry."

"Are you really going to stay four more years in the Legion?"

"Yes. I could desert, but I want to join their commando unit." He smiled at his mother. "Don't worry; I promise you, I'll come back without any bits missing."

His father drank some whisky and asked, "Have you thought about what you're going to do after you leave the Legion?"

"Yes, I'm going to join the police."

Adele smiled. "I'm glad you're coming back to England, even if we do have to wait another four years."

His father went to the drinks cabinet. "I'm very pleased with your decision; let's all have another drink. I will be glad to see more of you. Your mother is not the only one that misses you. What made you think of the police? You've never spoken about it before."

Ransome took a few minutes to reply. "It seems an interesting job without too many dull moments, and I quite like the idea of crime prevention and criminal investigation. I would like to be a detective like you."

Adele got up. "While you're all having a chat, I'm going to put the dinner on." She looked at her son. "You're not going to go hungry in this house."

Later, while they were eating, Ransome brought them up-to-date with his activities in the Legion and explained what it was like in the 2nd REP.

"You know, John, with your gift for foreign languages, your ability in martial arts and your Legion experience, you could join MI6."

"You must be joking, Dad. They work for the government, and all I feel for the government is complete contempt. The police are not without blemish, but I would prefer to join them."

A few days later, Ransome was having breakfast with his father. "Dad, what's the latest on Billy Mays and his girlfriend, Lynne Fairfield?"

"I didn't know you were interested in London gangsters."

"I'm not really, but my best friend Alan is." He explained Alan's involvement with Lynne.

"Mays and his men smuggle drugs into England. Most of the drugs sold in London come from him and we've been trying to get him for a long time, but no one will testify against him; witnesses are intimidated, or murdered. I advise your friend not to return to London or to contact Lynne until he is brought to justice."

The time went by quickly, and all too soon his leave was over. On the last day, he bid farewell to his parents and sister, and left for France.

BACK FROM LEAVE

When Ransome arrived back in barracks, he spoke to Alan.

"My father says Billy is still too powerful and dangerous. London is still too hot for you, it's not time to return yet, but his luck has to run out sometime."

"Yeah, but when?"

In their third year, Ransome and Alan went on a corporals' course at Castelnaudary. After they completed it and passed, they applied to join the Reconnaissance Commandos of the CEA. Before being accepted they had to pass some tough physical tests, but once those were over they started their training. Because the commandos go on difficult missions their training is harder than that of other units, and includes HALO (high altitude low opening) parachute jumping. The commandos have a proud history and have seen service in many countries, including Gabon, Kuwait, Lebanon and Iraq. They acted as bodyguards to Yassir Arafat when he had to leave Beirut in 1982, and they rescued the Prime Minister of Rwanda when he was being held by the Rwandan Army in 1994.

In the commandos, Ransome and Alan were always on the move. If they weren't on a mission, there was always more training. The commandos were on-call to go anywhere at any time, and during one of their missions, Alan saved Ransome's life.

HOSTAGES

The call came at 10.00 a.m. Gilles Lacasse, the French Commissioner in Djibouti, was in his office dictating a letter to his secretary. She picked up the phone and said, "Hello, High Commissioner's office."

"I must speak to the Commissioner."

"Sir, Colonel Dubois is on the line."

"Hello. Marc, what's up?"

"We have a problem. A school bus carrying thirty French children has been seized by six terrorists. They shot dead the driver, but one of our Puma helicopters intercepted the bus and bought it to a halt. It's now near the Somali border, and there are two army trucks parked in front of it to prevent it going any further."

"Any idea what they want?"

"No, but they want you to negotiate with them."

"What units have you got on the scene?"

"A company of paratroopers. I've also sent for the Legion's Elite Commando Unit. We have a helicopter waiting for you at Djibouti Airport."

"Good, I'm leaving now."

In the car on the way to the airport he was in a

thoughtful mood. He was an ambitious man, but this business looked tricky, and if things turned out badly they would be looking for a scapegoat. He arrived at the airport twenty minutes later and boarded the helicopter. It was hot, so he opened a bottle of water. He could not get used to the heat and hoped his next posting would be back in Europe.

After a short journey, the helicopter landed well away from the bus. A Jeep drove up and Colonel Dubois got out.

"What's the latest situation, Marc?"

"Nothing much has changed. They call themselves 'Le Front de Liberation de Djibouti' and want to overthrow the government. We've established a radio link with them."

They both got into the Jeep and were driven to the border post. When they arrived, the commissioner spoke to the terrorists.

"This is the High Commissioner."

A response came over the radio. "Ah, Commissioner, my name is Mohammad Rahman. We demand the release of our leader Abdullah Bassam and five of our men by 1800 hours tomorrow. If that does not happen, we will kill all the children. If you comply with our demands, all of them will be released."

"I will inform my superiors of your demands and get back to you," the commissioner said. "You heard that, Marc. I think their terms are unacceptable. Their acts of terrorism have gone on too long; the children will have to be rescued. I'm going to report back. When will the commandos arrive?"

"In about ten hours."

Later that afternoon, the terrorists allowed Mademoiselle Rousseau, the director of the primary school, onto the bus; food and water were also delivered. Meanwhile, in Calvi, Ransome's unit was on the firing range when they were told to return to barracks. There, Captain Lambert, the leader of the unit, gave a briefing and told them they were going to Djibouti to rescue children who were being held hostage on a school bus. After getting their weapons, they were taken to the airport where they boarded a plan for Djibouti.

Inside the aircraft, they sat down on canvas seats, but their parachutes prevented them from being comfortable. The engines started, and the plane moved along the tarmac and took to the air. Although there was a lot of noise from the engines, Ransome shut his eyes and tried to get some sleep. Hours later, the side door opened, a red light flashed, then turned green, and the jumpmaster shouted "Debout, accrochez."

They stood up, made their way to the open door and jumped into the cold night. They landed near the border post, where they were met by a lieutenant who took Captain Lambert to see Colonel Dubois while the unit stayed near the post.

After Captain Lambert had been briefed by the colonel, he deployed his men around the bus. Two of them would keep it under observation with infrared binoculars while the others slept. The next morning, the commissioner had a meeting with the colonel.

"Paris will not give in to their demands. Have you got a rescue plan?"

"Yes, we need to convince the terrorists that their leader and his men will be released and arrive here at 1700 hours. We also need you to ask them to allow food and drink to be delivered. The food will contain tranquilisers to send the children to sleep. Captain Lambert has deployed his men around the bus, all of whom have throat microphones. When the children fall asleep and the terrorists are visible, his snipers will shoot them while the rest of his men charge the bus and rescue the children; separately, a platoon of Legionnaires will attack the Somali machinegun position. We know that the Somalis support the terrorists and would help them if a rescue was attempted."

After their conversation, the commissioner contacted the terrorists and spoke to their leader.

"Paris has agreed to your terms, and Abdullah Bassam and five of his men will arrive today at 1700 hours by helicopter. When will you release the children and Mademoiselle Rousseau?"

"When our beloved leader and five of our brothers arrive and are set free, we will set all of the hostages free."

"The children must be hungry and thirsty; we need to send food and water as soon as possible."

"Yes, send it."

After the commissioner had finished talking to the terrorist leader, he turned to Colonel Dubois and said, "I hope this does not turn into a massacre, Marc."

"It's a dangerous situation, Commissioner, but Captain Lambert has full confidence in his men."

The colonel pulled out a packet of Gauloises, and they both lit up. They smoked and talked for a while; ten minutes later, the colonel left to give his orders. The food and water were delivered to the bus, and Mademoiselle Rousseau distributed it to the children, having previously been told that the food would be tranquilised. After the children had eaten and settled down, she pretended to fall asleep. Once the children were asleep and the terrorists were visible to the snipers, the order was given to shoot. Four of them were killed; the other two took cover and crouched below the windows. One of them was near the door, ready to kill anyone who entered. The other was preparing to kill the children, and with a short burst from his Uzi he killed a small boy. As he turned his weapon to kill more children, Mademoiselle Rousseau leapt up from her seat and tried to seize his submachine gun. As they struggled, the door of the bus was flung open and Beaumont, the First Commando, came in. He was immediately shot down by the terrorist guarding the door.

Ransome, who was following him, opened up with his Heckler submachine gun. As the dying terrorist fell, Ransome saw the other one knock down the primary school director and start to aim his Uzi at him; before he could pull the trigger, Ransome shot him dead. He helped Mademoiselle Rousseau to her feet. She wasn't badly hurt, and went round and calmed down the children who were shocked by the violence and death, and then led them off the bus. When the attack on the bus began, a platoon of Legionnaires attacked and destroyed the Somali machinegun post. Two of them were killed.

Afterwards, Captain Lambert spoke to his men.

"I congratulate you on your performance in the rescue of the children and the death of the terrorists. It is unfortunate that a small boy and three Legionnaires were killed, but in any hostage situation one cannot guarantee that everyone will be saved. We're all going back now for a well-earned rest."

Back in Calvi, Ransome and Alan decided to go for a drink in town with Sven and Marco, two friends from their unit. They didn't see much of Vic, Pete and Roger because they were in another regiment, although they kept in touch and saw them occasionally.

Sven bought the first round and asked, "Were you afraid, John?"

"No, I just wanted to kill the terrorists and get the children out. It's a pity about Beaumont; he was a good man. I'm glad I shot his killer and the other terrorist before he could murder any more children. Some men deserve to die."

LEAVING

It was getting close to the end of his five-year contract, and Ransome was talking to Alan about what he was going to do after he left the Legion.

"I'm not going to re-enlist; it's been a hard five years and I want to spend a couple of months with my family," Ransome said. "Then I'm going travelling, and when I get back I'm joining the police. What about you?"

"Since I don't have to re-enlist for another five years, I'll stay for a shorter time; sooner or later, Billy is going to wind up dead or in prison, and when that happens I'm going back to find Lynne."

A few months before his departure, Ransome was called to the colonel's office. He knocked on the door and went in.

"Ah, Ransome, I thought I would have a few words with you. The Legion does not like to lose experienced, well-trained men." He tried, without much success, to persuade Ransome to re-enlist, but in the end he said, "Are you sure you won't reconsider?"

"I'm afraid not, sir, I've made up my mind to go."

The evening before his last day, there was a party, and

Ransome was talking to his friends Sven and Marco.

"I thought you guys were leaving?"

"Not yet. We will stay on for another year; after that, who knows? Perhaps work as bodyguards."

Later, Alan joined the party, and as the beer flowed the friends reminisced about the last five years.

"John, you will let me know if anything happens to Billy, won't you?"

"Yeah, no problem. You miss Lynne, don't you?"

"Yes, I do."

Early the next morning, there was a parade, and those leaving were given a Certificate of Military Service.

A few days later, Ransome was back in London. During his five years in the Legion he had saved £9,000, so there was no rush to earn a crust. There was a party to welcome him back, and his relatives came to hear about his adventures in the Legion. He was enjoying his time off, seeing old friends and practising his karate.

A few days after the party, he was walking along Villers Street at 2.15 a.m. when, as he turned into John Adams Street, he saw two men. As he got closer, he saw a broad-shouldered youth threatening a thin, well-dressed middle-aged man with a large knife. He heard him say, "Give me your credit cards and your money, or you get a knife in the guts."

Ransome tapped him on the shoulder, and as he turned his head in surprise, he hit him and kept on hitting him until he dropped to the ground; then he knelt down beside him, picked up his knife and felt for a pulse.

"He will live, not that it matters very much," Ransome

told the man. "When he regains consciousness he can make his own way to hospital. It's best to give muggers a good beating rather then send them to jail. Now, apart from us the street is empty, so let's move away." He looked at the man. "You look very pale and shaken."

"Yes, it was very unexpected. I really don't know how to thank you for dealing with that thug."

"It was nothing, I needed the exercise."

"Look, it's late now. Come and have a drink at my hotel. I have a suite at the Radisson Edwardian – it's not far from here. Let me introduce myself; I'm Andrew Stellman of Stellman Oil. And you are?"

"John Ransome."

When they arrived at his hotel, they went up to his suite. Stellman produced a bottle of malt whisky and two glasses, and poured a generous amount into each. They sat down and Stellman began to talk.

"I had two bodyguards, but my car was involved in an accident yesterday and they were both injured and are in hospital. Last night, I couldn't sleep and went out for a walk to stretch my legs; in retrospect, not a wise decision."

"London can be a dangerous city, Mr Stellman."

"Please, call me Andrew. Tell me about yourself, John. What have you been doing for the last few years?"

"I was in the French Foreign Legion for five years. Now I'm having a break and spending some time with my family. Next month, I'm going abroad for a while, and when I get back I'm going to join the police. After I leave the police, I want to set up my own security firm."

They continued talking, and Ransome told him in more detail about his time in the Legion and the commando unit, after which he said, "Thanks for the drink, Andrew. I'll be off now."

"John, why don't stay in the hotel and have a good sleep? I'll phone down to reception and get you a room. Tomorrow, we can have a late breakfast."

"That might not be a bad idea."

After the call was made, Ransome said, "Thanks, Andrew, I'll see you tomorrow."

AKIRA

He left Stellman and went down to the reception to get his key. When he arrived at his room, he took a shower and then went to bed. An hour later, there was a knock on his door.

"Room service."

He opened the door, standing there was a beautiful young Chinese girl who said, with an impish grin, "My name is Akira. Mr Stellman sent me; he said after your exercise you might need a massage."

Ransome smiled. "Yeah; who am I to argue with Mr Stellman? Come in."

Once inside, she said, "I'm going to give you a topless massage."

He smiled. "Only a massage?" He looked at her as she took off her top.

She was tall, with a shapely figure, long legs and medium-sized breasts. As she was massaging him, he became erect. There was too much lust and passion for Ransome to get any sleep that night. He was tired but happy when he went up to Stellman's suite for a late breakfast the next morning. He thought Akira was a sensational girl and had got her phone number.

"What do you want for breakfast, John?"

"Steak, egg and chips."

"Did you get a good rest?"

Ransome smiled. "Not with Akira, she was insatiable. I haven't felt this good for a long time. Thanks for sending her along."

After they had finished eating, Stellman got the bottle of malt out and, as they were drinking, he said, "I'm going to need a couple of bodyguards. Have you any contacts, John?"

"Yes, Craig – he runs a security company. Do you want me to call him?"

"Yes."

Ransome made the call.

"Craig?"

"Ah, John, you've decided to take the job."

"No, but thanks for the offer. I'm with Andrew Stellman of Stellman Oil. He needs a couple of bodyguards on the quick. Have you anybody available?"

"Yeah, I've got two ex-SAS guys. What's your address?"

After Craig had written it down, he said, "They will be with you in two hours. I'm impressed, John, you mixing with the big shots."

"Yeah, that's another story. Thanks, Craig."

After the call, Stellman told Ransome about his early life and how he had started his oil company. When the bodyguards arrived, Ransome got ready to leave, and Stellman gave him an envelope and said, "Something for your trip abroad."

"Thanks, Andrew."

"Let's stay in touch. After you've got your firm going

I might be able to put some work your way."

"That won't be for a few years yet, but thanks for the offer, Andrew." He shook hands with him and left.

Ransome kept in contact with Stellman, and whenever he came to London they would see each other and go for a drink or to a restaurant. Stellman admired Ransome because he was a man of action, unlike his son who was weak and indecisive.

When he got home, he opened the envelope and saw that there was a cheque for £5,000 inside. He hadn't expected Stellman to be so generous.

The next day he phoned Akira.

"Hi, it's John. I'm going on holiday next month for two weeks. Can you come with me?"

She laughed. "But you've only known me for one night."

"Yeah, well, let's just say I was intoxicated by your charms. So what's your answer?"

"Tell you what, take me to an expensive restaurant and we will talk about it."

She went with him on holiday, and when they returned she became his girlfriend. He bought a second-hand car and they started to look for a flat to rent. When they found one, she moved in with him. His mother wasn't happy when he moved out, but it was bound to happen sooner or later. After they had arranged the flat as they wanted it, he joined the Metropolitan Police and started his training at Hendon. Akira thought the job was dangerous and tried to persuade him not to join, but he had made up his mind.

JOINING THE POLICE

After weeks of training and a parade, Ransome was ready to start work as a police officer. His first posting was to Walthamstow Police Station he arrived there one Monday morning with three other police officers, looking smart in their new uniforms. They were given a pep talk by a senior officer, who told them that "When the Metropolitan Police was formed on 19 September 1829 it had 1,000 officers; now there were 31,000 patrolling 609 square miles. As for the work schedule, there's an early shift from 6 a.m. to 2 p.m., and a late shift from 2 p.m. to 10 p.m. The night duty is from 10 p.m. to 6 a.m."

He continued his talk, giving other information about the force, and when he had finished they went down to the canteen for tea.

Because Ransome was a rookie, for the first two weeks he went on patrol with an experienced officer named Tim Morris, who taught him how to deal with the public and the 'incidents' that occurred everyday.

On the last day of their patrol together, Morris asked, "What do you think of the job, John?"

"Not bad, something different everyday. After five

years in the Legion and the things I've done there, I'm confident I can handle any situation that comes along."

He successfully completed his two-year probationary period and, a couple of years later, decided to advance his career. He passed an exam and was promoted to sergeant, and was posted to Twickenham. There, he became a custody officer. It was a job he didn't find interesting. He had heard about SO19, the Armed Response Unit, and sent off an application form. Some weeks later, he was summoned for an interview in Old Street. It went well, and a few weeks later he went to Lippitts Hill for firearms training, not that he really needed it. The standard weapons used by the armed response units are the Heckler & Koch MP5 and the Glock 17, which both use the same 9mm ammunition. Other weapons are available, such as the Remington 870 pump-action shotgun. He did not find the training hard, as he already knew how to use all the guns.

After the course had finished, they gathered in the old gymnasium to find out if they had passed. He didn't think there was even a remote chance that he had failed. It had become very quiet as they sat and waited for their names to be called. The first one to be called returned with a glum look on his face, and the second came back looking even more despondent; after him, there were some who had been successful. At last, he heard his own name called.

He walked down the corridor, knocked on the last door and went in. Seated behind the desk was Superintendent Lock, whom he had met before, and two other officers, whom he did not recognise, standing next to him.

“Ah, Ransome, the last man on the list. Sit down.” He looked at some papers in front of him. “Congratulations, you’ve done very well; you’ve passed.”

“Thank you, sir.”

After he left the office, he phoned Akira.

“Put your best dress on. I’ve passed, and we are going out to celebrate when I get back.”

The next few months were busy. Operating from Old Street, Ransome put together a good team. Their call sign was Tango 800, and as the jobs came in thick and fast they gained a lot of experience.

TOTTENHAM

It was a very cold October morning. Jerry was driving the Armed Response vehicle down Tottenham High Street. As they were passing Lloyds Bank, they saw two men coming out; one was carrying a large holdall.

Jerry said, "Sarge, I recognise them. Clem Terrace and George Manning have both done time for armed robbery with violence."

Jerry stopped the vehicle a short distance from the bank and he and Ransome jumped out, followed closely by Len who had been sitting in the back. They were armed with Heckler & Koch 9mm carbines, except for Len who carried a Glock 17 pistol. They had seen the robbers cross the High Street and run down the side road opposite the bank. As they chased them, Jerry shouted, "Stop, armed police."

They saw them get into a waiting car, and the driver, on seeing the approaching police, pulled out a pistol and opened fire. He missed, and Ransome shot him dead. Terrace and Manning had also drawn their guns and were firing at the police officers. Len went down, hit by two bullets in the leg. As the bullets spattered around them, Ransome and Jerry returned fire. Ransome shot Terrace in the forehead; Jerry's burst wounded Manning in the shoulder. Afterwards, Ransome attended to Len, who was lying on the ground, trying to stop the bleeding from his right leg.

"Hang on, Len, the ambulance will soon be here."

"Yeah, it bloody hurts. It's just not my lucky day."

Meanwhile, Jerry was dealing with Manning, who was squealing with pain from his shoulder wound. Both he and Len were taken to the hospital, and Jerry went with them. Other units soon arrived and cordoned off the crime scene. The bodies of the getaway driver and Terrace were taken away, and £25,000 was found in the holdall. Later that evening, Ransome went to see Len in hospital.

The next day, he learned from detectives who had questioned the bank staff after the robbery that Terrace and Manning, armed with pistols, had taken a young mother and her son hostage, and threatened to shoot them unless they were given money.

CID

His two years in the Armed Response Unit had been exciting, with many call-outs, but he felt it was time for a change. He was interested in investigating crime and applied for the Criminal Investigation Department (CID). He knew this was not going to be easy: many applied, few were chosen. He informed his superiors and his name was put on a list. To get in, he would be up against other officers and would need to be interviewed to assess his suitability for the job. On the day of the interview, he arrived at 10.00 a.m. at City Road Police Station and sat with the others in a small room. The interviews were to be held in a meeting room. Eventually, his name was called and he went into the room. Inside were three men, and there was a chair in the middle of the room.

Ransome said, “Good morning, gentlemen.”

Commander Williams, who was in charge of the proceedings, said, “Sit down, Mr Ransome.” He had his file in front of him. “We are impressed with your record so far and your work in the Armed Response Unit.”

What followed were questions, lots of them, about his background and family, about the law, police procedure, the courts, warrants, informants and what he would do if he saw an officer taking a bribe. Ransome's experience and the fact he had done his homework meant he was well prepared. Finally, the interview came to an end.

"Thank you, Mr Ransome. That will be all. Have you any questions?"

"No, sir, and thank you, gentlemen." He thought the interview had gone well.

Soon, he learnt that his application had been successful, and he began work as a detective in Shoreditch. The CID office was kept busy investigating robberies, shootings, burglaries, murders and rapes. After a murder, he would make house-to-house calls, gathering evidence, interrogating suspects and making arrests. He also built up a list of informants; one of the best was Charlie Dunsten. Ransome had brought him in for questioning about a break-in.

"Look, Charlie, on the evidence I have I can charge you with the burglary at Latimar Road, or I can let you go. It's up to you. I need information."

Dunsten didn't say anything for a while, but then said, "There's a guy selling guns in Hackney."

He gave Ransome a name and an address. It was a good tip, which led to an arrest and the recovery of five handguns, two sawn-off shotguns and some ammunition.

On another occasion, when Dunsten was giving him a tip, Ransome said, "Charlie, I know you're not big-time, but if you ever get any information about Billy Mays, let me know."

He found the job interesting and, as his career progressed, he was promoted to Detective Inspector.

BILLY MAYS

Billy Mays owned a large house in Hampstead. He was a casually dressed, tall, broad-shouldered man with closely cropped black hair handsome, in a dangerous kind of way. He kept himself very fit and looked younger than his forty years. He had been a criminal ever since he left school; starting off as a mugger, he then tried burglary and eventually drifted into drug dealing. Later, he made his fortune by importing huge amounts of drugs into Britain. He had been to prison when he was younger, but only for a year. The police knew about his activities but could never pin anything on him; witnesses were bribed, or murdered, and nobody was stupid enough to inform on him as they knew what would happen.

He had summoned his men to a meeting, and seated at the head of a large table in his lounge, Billy began to speak.

"We're getting a lot of grief! Those fuckers from the drug squad are getting right up my arse. Over the last five years we've made millions, so we're not short of money. It's time to close down for a while. We're all going down to Marbella for six months; of course, the coppers are going to find out where we are, but there's no law against drinking, sunbathing or fucking the local pussy. While we're relaxing, Tommy is going to be setting a job up for us: a kidnapping. This should bring in a good few million. Lynne and I are going to Spain in a couple of days. We're staying at the Marbella Club Hotel, and I expect you lot in Marbella within two weeks. Now, let's have some booze and play some poker!"

After he had been in Marbella for a few weeks, Billy bought a villa. During this time, Ransome got a phone call from his friend in the drug squad, Mickey Prince.

"Hello, John. I've got news about Billy Mays. He's in Marbella with his men; he's bought a villa there. I think things were getting too hot for him in London so he decided to get out. How long he will be there, I don't know. I will keep you posted."

"Thanks a lot, Mickey, I appreciate it."

The next time Alan phoned, Ransome informed him about Billy.

"John, I will be on leave soon. Maybe I should go to Marbella and kill him!"

"Leave it for a while, Alan. You will get him, but when you do I want to be there backing you up."

It was difficult, but Ransome managed to persuade him not to go. After five months had passed, Billy was getting restless, the clubs, the sun and Spain were getting on his nerves; he wanted action. So he was more than happy when Tommy phoned and said the job was on. After his call, Billy shouted out of his villa window to a group of men sunbathing near the swimming pool.

"Nick, come up here for a minute. Listen, the job's

on. I want you to contact Enrico. I want to use his boat to get us back to England. We need to land on that quiet stretch of beach where he smuggled the drugs. Tommy will pick us up there; I don't want the police to know we're back in the UK."

Back in England, Tommy had been looking for a detached house for Billy and his men, and a flat for Lynne. Tommy was Tommy Smart, a bent copper who was suspected of being corrupt; although nothing was ever proven. He decided to leave the force shortly afterwards and joined a detective agency run by a friend. While in the police, he had done some jobs for Billy and tipped him off about some raids, and was well rewarded for his trouble. When Billy and his men arrived, Tommy took them to the detached house in Redhill that he had rented for Billy under an assumed name.

Later, when they were both sitting down having a drink, Tommy asked, "Is Lynne's flat okay?"

"Yeah, she likes it, and it's not too far from here; more importantly, if the cops discover this address, we've got her flat to hide in, it's big enough. Now, another thing I need a replacement for is George; he was killed in Marbella. The stupid fucker was drunk and crashed his car into a lorry."

"Have you got anyone in mind?"

"Yeah," Tommy said, "I might have. There's Steve Rim; he's been involved in armed robbery, but they couldn't prove it. He's done some time for grievous bodily harm. He's a tough bastard, but smart enough. I'll send him round."

Later, Billy's men were in the lounge sitting around a table playing poker. The air was thick with cigar smoke, and bottles of whisky and cans of lager were on the table. Billy was sitting behind a desk smoking a cigar, dressed in an expensive dark suit, white shirt and dark tie; the watch on his wrist was a Rolex. At four o'clock, Rim arrived and was shown in. He was a big man, and he wore a black baseball hat, white T-shirt, jeans and trainers.

Billy looked at him in disgust and said, "What the fuck are you supposed to be? You look like a lavatory cleaner; didn't Tommy tell you to dress smart? What do you think I'm running here, a fucking cleaning firm?"

Billy opened a drawer in his desk and took out a wad of notes, peeled off some fifties, and said, "Nick, take this money and go with him to make sure he returns looking smart."

When they returned, he said to Rim, "I've got a few rules; two of them are, don't fuck your head up with drugs and drink only what you can handle. We've been successful so far, and I intend it to stay that way. I don't like mistakes!"

Late in the evening, he began to discuss the kidnapping with his men.

"The target is Sir Donald Grey and his wife Samantha. They have been married for ten years. He is fifty, his wife thirty. She used to be a fashion model and is still a nice piece of ass. They live in a six-bedroom detached house in Enfield. They have two sons. The plan is to snatch the wife as she is on her way home from dropping off the kids at a private school. Grey is worth £100 million. For the safe return of his wife, we want £10 million. I will use her mobile to contact him. The money will be paid into a numbered Swiss bank account, and when the money has been transferred, we will release the wife and fly to Zurich in a private jet to get the money. Every Monday, she follows the same routine: she drives her kids to school and then returns home. At twelve o'clock, her friends come round for a drink and to play cards. We will follow her car, ambush it and snatch the wife. It won't take long, and we'll all be wearing masks."

LYNNE

A few days before the kidnapping, Ransome was in his office in Shoreditch when Mickey rang.

"John?"

"Yes."

"I have some new information on Lynne Fairfield. Billy Mays' girlfriend was spotted shopping in Knightsbridge by one of my men, and he followed her to a flat near Redhill. We watched the flat for some time, but Billy never showed."

"Do you have the address?"

After he had provided the address, Mickey said, "Oh, by the way, she is using another name: Eleanor Winters."

"Thanks, Mickey. I owe you a drink."

Mickey laughed. "More than one, John."

He decided to go and see her that evening. Billy and his men were dangerous, so when he arrived outside her block of flats he carried a Glock 17 pistol in a shoulder holster he had bought from one of his contacts. He spoke to her on the intercom.

"Eleanor Winters?"

"Yes."

"I'm Detective Inspector John Ransome. I would like to ask you some questions."

"About what?"

"I would prefer to discuss that in your flat."

He was allowed to go up. He was a tall, handsome, well-built man with light-blonde hair and blue eyes. He was dressed in a smart grey suit, and from a distance he looked like a businessman, but when he came up close one realised this was no businessman; he looked too tough, his eyes had a certain look of careless menace and he was not the type to fool around with. He took the lift to the fourth floor and walked a short distance to her flat. He knocked on the door and she opened it. After showing his warrant card, she led him into the reception. She was a very attractive, slim and barefooted blonde. She was about thirty but didn't look it. She wore a yellow blouse and a short black skirt; it was easy to see why Alan had fallen for her.

She said politely, "Would you like to sit down?"

Ransome didn't sit down; instead, he drew his gun and checked every room of the large flat. After he was satisfied there was no one there, he put his gun away and sat down.

By this time, Lynne was furious and shouted, "Who the hell do you think you are, searching my flat and waving a gun around?"

"I'm looking for your boyfriend, Billy Mays."

"Never heard of him. I'm Eleanor Winters."

"Look, let's cut out the nonsense, shall we?"

"You're Lynne Fairfield. Where is your boyfriend, Billy Mays?"

"Well, as you can see, Inspector, he's not here. I don't know where he is, and I don't know when he's coming."

Ransome didn't really expect to get anything out of her. He didn't speak for a few minutes, and then said, "Alan is coming to London." He was amazed at the change in her expression. The hard tough look vanished, and her face became soft and gentle.

She said in almost a whisper, "You know Alan?"

"Yes."

She had been standing, but now she sat down. She seemed to be in a bit of a daze, her mind was in turmoil. She hadn't seen Alan for over nine years and had lost touch with him. Their affair had only ended because Billy found out about it and tried to have him killed. She had learnt that Tommy Smart, a corrupt police officer, had helped Billy to find him. If Alan was coming to London, Billy would try to kill him again. She remembered what Billy had said when he had found out about them – 'You've had your fling, now it's over. You will never see him again.' He never hit her, he didn't have to. If he had succeeded in killing Alan, that would have been the worst punishment of all.

She was quiet for ten minutes and then said, "How do I know you are telling the truth?"

"I'm not lying, Lynne; we served in the French Foreign Legion together. After five years I left and he stayed; he spoke about you many times. He can't get you out of his mind and says he has to see you again. He's my best friend, he saved my life. When I found out Billy was in Marbella, I told Alan and he wanted to go there and kill him. He's on leave now, and I have invited him to stay with my girlfriend and me in our flat. I wanted to keep him out of trouble, but that no longer looks possible. Has Billy been here?"

"No. He said he will be here in a few days."

"Do you know where he is staying with his men, or what they are planning?"

"No."

"If you give me your mobile number, Alan will phone you in two days' time when he arrives in London; until then, stay in the flat. One way or another, Billy is not going to be around for much longer."

After he left, she poured herself a drink and sat down. She no longer loved Billy, but he wasn't the kind of man she could walk out on. Memories of the good times she had with Alan came flooding back. She wanted him, and she didn't know how she had survived without him all those years. She went to bed late but didn't sleep very much.

Later, Ransome phoned an uncle of his who owned a small hotel in Ilford.

"Paul, a friend of mine and his girlfriend need to stay in your hotel for a short time, but I don't want them to sign in the register; I would like to keep their visit quiet."

"Leave it with me, John. What are their names?"

"Alan Eastman and Lynne Fairfield."

"When are they coming?"

"In a couple of days. Thanks, Paul."

Alan arrived at King's Cross two days later. Leaving the station, he found a café and ordered a coffee. He had Lynne's number. Was it really nine years since he had last seen her? So much had happened since then. He could not stop thinking about her. There had been other women in his life, but somehow none could compare to her. He wanted her more than any other woman but wondered how she felt about him now. He hadn't liked leaving London because of Billy, but now he was back and determined to get him and, with John's help, this was more than just a possibility. He rang her number.

"Lynne?"

"Oh, Alan, is it really you?"

"Yes, I'm back in London, and this time I'm not leaving. It's been so long, Lynne, I just had to see you again."

"Where are you?"

"King's Cross, but I'm going to a small hotel in Ilford; John's booked me a room there."

"Can you give me the address?" She wrote it down and said, "I'm leaving now and will get there as soon as possible. I'll give you a ring when I'm near."

Alan took a taxi to the hotel and walked into the reception, where there was a short, fat man sitting behind the desk.

"Alan Eastman."

"Ah, yes, Mr Eastman, we were expecting you. There's no need to sign in."

He gave him a key and said, "Room number 10, it's on the second floor."

"Is there a bar here?"

"Yes, it's in the basement."

"Thank you." He went up to his room.

It was large and clean, with a comfortable double

bed. He unpacked his suitcase, and after taking a shower he went down to the bar. She arrived two and a half hours later and walked into the bar. She saw him sitting at a small table near the entrance. He was a good-looking man with brown eyes, of medium height and weight – he looked slimmer and fitter than she remembered. They looked at each other; then he got up and went over to her, and they started kissing. After pausing for breath, they went to the bar and bought some drinks.

He looked at her and said, "You're more beautiful than ever."

She smiled and said, "You're not looking bad yourself."

He took her hand and kissed it. "Lynne, you're the only woman I've ever wanted. I'm not leaving you this time. I'm staying in London. Billy will be taken care of."

They had some more drinks and carried on talking for a long time until she said, "Let's go to your room and make up for lost time."

Once inside, she took her clothes off. She still had that slim, sexy body with the firm breasts and long legs that drove him crazy with lust and passion. He stripped off, and they got on the bed and started to make love. After he came good and hard inside her, she cuddled up to him and said, "It's always so good with you. What do you think about us having some kids?"

"With you? Yeah, I'd like that very much."

As they lay on the bed, he asked, "Have you any idea where Billy and his men are?"

"No, but a bent copper called Tommy Smart might know. He's the one who was helping him find you and rented a flat for me."

They talked a bit more, and then made love again.

They got up late the next morning and went down for breakfast. As they were eating, he said, "We'll stay here for a few days. I'll let John know about Smart this morning; perhaps he can find out what he knows. I'll phone him when we get back to our room."

After receiving Alan's call, Ransome began looking to see what he could get on Smart. He found out that he was suspected of taking bribes and helping major criminals to evade justice by selling secret information about police operations. He had left the force and now worked for a private detective agency run by a friend of his. Smart maintained contacts with other corrupt officers and could obtain information from the Police National Computer.

Later that evening, Ransome phoned Alan.

"Listen, Alan, tomorrow night I'm going to Smart's flat to see if I can find out where Mays is staying."

"Okay, John, I'll wait to hear from you."

Late the following night, Ransome went down to Smart's flat in East London. He parked his car at the end of the road and then walked to his ground-floor flat. It was in darkness, and making sure no one was about he used a jemmy to break in. One of the rooms was being used as a home office, and had a desk with a computer. He searched the desk and found details of two properties. One was for Lynne's flat; the other was a semi-detached house in Redhill that had been rented to a Sean Jennings. He thought that must be where Billy and his men were staying. He wrote down the address and left.

KIDNAPPING

On Monday morning, Samantha Grey dropped off her sons at school and drove away. Two cars that had been parked on the opposite side of the road followed her. Nick was driving the first car, a BMW, with Billy sitting next to him; Steve was in the back.

Billy spoke to them. "Right, she is going home the usual way; it will take about forty minutes. When we reach that quiet road, and I think the time is right, we'll put our masks on. Nick, you will overtake her and swing the wheel to the left to block her passage, making sure that you leave enough distance for her to brake."

After twenty minutes, Billy said, "Do it now!"

Nick followed his instructions and overtook her silver Audi, turned left and stopped in front of her. Samantha managed to brake just in time, stopping her car a few yards from theirs. Tony and Eric, who were behind her in the Mercedes and were masked, pulled up and got out. Tony pointed a Smith & Wesson 38 revolver at the terrified woman and said, "Out the car."

She got out of the car and fainted, as the shock of it all had been too much for her.

Billy, who had been watching the road, shouted, "Coppers coming!"

As the police car got closer, the two officers could see three stationary cars and masked men standing near a body lying in the road.

Billy drew his gun and shouted, "Let them have it!"

They shot the officers at point-blank range. Billy looked at Samantha lying in the road.

"Tony, Eric, tie her up, gag her, then blindfold her and put her in the boot of your car." He turned to Steve. "You will follow us in her Audi. Now, let's all get back to the house."

On their way back from the kidnapping, they were spotted by Charlie Dunsten who was in Enfield looking for houses to burgle. He saw them when their cars stopped at some traffic lights. Back in the house, Billy was giving orders.

"Nick, Steve, you will be looking after her, getting her meals, making sure she doesn't get away. There are bars on her windows, but always keep her door locked, keep your masks on when you see her and no funny stuff. I think her husband will pay the money – he's worth £100,000,000 – and when he does, we will return her in good condition. I don't want her touched. I'm going to phone him later on."

It was 4.00 p.m. and Sir Donald Grey was back home. He was worried because he hadn't heard from his wife all day, and the school had phoned him to get someone to pick up his sons. They were a close couple and she would usually ring him at least twice a day. She didn't answer her mobile and he had phoned all the places she could have been, but no one had seen her. As he pondered his next move, the phone rang.

"Donald?"

"Samantha?"

Billy tore the mobile from her hand. "Grey, listen, and listen good. We have your wife. She is unharmed. We want money for her safe return – £10,000,000. If we don't get it, you will not see her again. I'll phone you back in an hour. Don't do anything stupid like contact the police, we will know if you do." The phone went dead.

After the call to Grey, Billy spoke to his men. "You all heard that; we'll give him an hour to think things over, then I'll call him again, I'm sure he'll pay. Tommy is coming later."

Grey was devastated by the news of his wife's kidnapping; £10,000,000 was a huge sum of money, but he could not live without her. He thought of going to the police, but he didn't have much confidence in them. He was deep in thought when the phone rang again.

"You paying the money?"

"Yes, but don't hurt her."

"That won't happen as long as you pay the money. Listen, you will transfer £10 million to this bank account at 09.00 a.m. tomorrow morning." He gave him the details of the account, and then asked, "Have you got all that?"

"Yes."

"After we confirm the money is in the account, we will release your wife. We will leave her unharmed outside Manor House tube station at 12.30 p.m."

"How do I know you won't kill her and keep the money?"

"You don't, but I'm of the old school; if I give my word, I keep it. You send the money, she goes free. Just send the money and you will see your wife tomorrow."

Grey was shaking as he put the phone down. Billy was ecstatic after the call, and was in the lounge with his men standing around him.

"I knew he was going to pay; we'll soon be getting our money." He turned to Nick. "I'm going out for a few hours."

After he had left, his men got some drinks and put on a film. Twenty minutes later, Steve got up, picked up the keys to Samantha's bedroom and went upstairs. Nick followed him.

"What are you up to, Steve?"

"I'm going to have her; you can have a go when I've finished."

"You know what Billy said; he didn't want her touched."

"Yeah, but he's not here, and she's not going to tell him." Steve unlocked the door and went in.

Nick took out his mobile and phoned Billy.

"Steve's gone into her room; he's going to rape her."

"Just can't do what he's told, eh? Kill him," Billy ordered.

Nick put on his mask, pulled out his gun and went into the bedroom. He shot Steve twice in the back of the head. As he pulled Steve's body off Samantha, he said, "He was a stupid bastard. I never did like him." He dragged his body out of the bedroom, locked the door, put him in the next room and went downstairs.

When he returned to the others, Tony asked him, "Where's Steve?"

"He's dead. He was going to rape her, so Billy told me to kill him."

DEALING WITH BILLY

On the day of the kidnapping, Ransome was in his flat watching the early afternoon news on television. The main story was that two police officers had been murdered in Enfield. Then the phone rang; it was Dunsten.

"Mr Ransome, I've got some important information on the man you're interested in, but it's going to cost you a thousand."

"If it's good, Charlie, you'll get your money. I'll see you in two hours in the place where we last met."

It was a small pub in Harrow, and Dunsten was already there when he arrived. There were only a few drinkers inside and nobody took any notice of them. Dunsten started talking quietly.

"It was about 10.30 a.m. and I was in Enfield, walking past a set of traffic lights, when I happened to glance inside some cars that were waiting for the lights to change. Guess who was inside?' He whispered the name Billy Mays and his men.

"Are you sure it was him?"

"Yeah, definitely, no mistake."

Ransome took out an envelope. "There's a thousand in there," he said, "It's my own money. Don't talk about this to anyone."

"Don't worry, Mr Ransome; if Billy found out that I'd talked to a copper he would have me killed."

After Dunsten left the pub, he bought a malt and sat there thinking. The fact that Mays and his men were in Enfield at about the time that two police officers were murdered made them strong suspects. He knew that he should pass the information on to his superiors, but he wasn't going to. He finished his drink, left the pub and drove to Alan's hotel. When he arrived, he stayed inside the car and phoned Alan on his mobile.

"Alan, I'm in my car outside the hotel. I have to talk to you."

"Okay, I'll see you in five minutes."

When Alan arrived, Ransome relayed what Dunsten had told him and then said, "You saved my life, Alan, and I promised you I would help you deal with Billy. I found two addresses in Smart's flat. One was for Lynne's place; the other was for a semi-detached house in Redhill. We'll go there tonight and wipe Mays and his men out. They have evaded justice for too long. I will be back here at 9.30 p.m. to pick you up."

When Ransome returned that evening, Alan was already waiting. He got in the car and they drove off.

"Listen, Alan, I've got two holdall bags in the boot; each one contains a HKMP7A1 silenced submachine gun with night-sight and flashlight, plus three extended 40-round magazines. There's also a Glock 17 pistol."

They arrived after midnight. They saw the house from

the road, parked the car in a nearby street, took their holdalls from the boot and then climbed over the fence. The area around the house was paved, and there were three cars parked near the entrance. In the rear garden there was a variety of trees and shrubs. They put on their masks and took out their weapons. They broke into the house through the patio door of the dining room and waited five minutes to see if anyone had heard their entry. Nobody came, so they opened the inside door and walked down the passage. The first room they approached was the kitchen. The door was slightly ajar and they could see a light on. Smart was inside making himself a snack. Ransome pushed the door open and Alan went in. Smart looked very surprised as Alan pumped him with bullets. Leaving the kitchen, they walked a bit further and stopped outside a door that was also slightly ajar. Alan pushed it open and they burst into the lounge. Billy was at the bar mixing himself a drink his men were watching television. There were looks of sheer disbelief on their faces when Ransome and Alan burst in. As the gangsters tried to draw their guns, they were shot dead. Billy just managed to draw his pistol before Alan riddled him with bullets.

Afterwards, Ransome said, "Let's search their pockets and see if they yield any useful information."

After they'd finished, he said, "I've found a bunch of keys, two mobiles and a piece of paper with what looks like details of a foreign bank account in Billy's pockets. What have you found?"

"Wallets, mobile phones and cash."

"Let's check the other rooms."

They found nothing else of interest in the rooms

downstairs. Upstairs there were four bedrooms and a bathroom, and in one of the bedrooms was the body of a man who had been shot twice in the head. The room next to the bathroom was locked. Ransome tried Billy's keys and opened the door. As soon as Samantha heard the door being unlocked she became very frightened. Two men walked in, dressed in black, wearing masks and carrying submachine guns. Ransome asked, "Who are you?"

"Samantha Gray."

"Wife of the industrialist?"

"Yes. I was abducted after dropping the children off at school. They asked my husband to send £10,000,000 to a Swiss bank account for my release."

"You are safe now. We are going to let you go." He looked at Alan. "Stay with her. I'm going to get Billy's mobiles." He didn't want Samantha to see the dead bodies in the lounge. When Ransome returned with Billy's mobiles, he said, "Is one of these yours?"

"Yes."

"Phone your husband and tell him you have been rescued and will be back in three or four hours."

"Donald? I've been rescued and will be back in three or four hours."

"Thank God, Samantha, I've been going out of my mind with worry."

They talked a bit more, and after she had finished her call she said to Ransome and Alan, "Thank you very much for rescuing me. I wasn't sure if I would ever leave this house alive. What has happened to the kidnappers?"

"They are all dead. The reason we are still wearing

our masks is that we don't want to be identified. Now, if you give us your address, we will take you home."

They left the house and went to the cars parked outside.

Ransome asked her, "Is one of these cars yours?"

"Yes, the silver Audi,' Samantha replied.

"I will drive you home, but you will have to go in the boot, I'm afraid; because I will have to take my mask off before I drive the car. Alan, you follow in the Mercedes."

When they arrived at her house, Ransome put his mask back on and helped her out of the boot. They watched as she ran to the house and saw her husband open the door. They returned to Billy's house.

The following night there was a massive explosion and fire at the house. The police found some bodies, but they were too badly burnt to be identified. A number of criminals were questioned about the murders of the two police officers in Enfield, but none were charged. During the investigation, an anonymous call was received by the officer in charge of the investigation, and the caller said that the bodies found in the house in Redhill were those of Billy Mays and his men, and it was they who had murdered the two officers because they had been witnesses to a kidnapping. The police weren't entirely convinced that the story was true because no kidnapping had been reported, but Mays and his men were never seen again. The investigation ended without a satisfactory conclusion; no arrests were made.

After the attack on the house, Alan returned to Lynne and told her what had happened.

"John and I went to the house in Redhill that Billy

and his men were using. They are all dead now. I think it was always going to happen this way. In the house we found a prisoner, a woman, the wife of an industrialist. She was being held for a ransom, but we released her and took her home to her husband."

Lynne kissed him and said, "I'm so glad you got back safely. Now sit down and I'll get you a drink."

"You know, Lynne, now we can start making plans for our future. When my leave is over I shall return to the Legion, but in three months' time I can leave and we can get married."

NAGGING FEELING

A month later, Ransome was having a drink with his friend, Mickey Prince, in a pub on Edgware Road. They were discussing the murder of the two police officers in Enfield.

"Not a good result, John, two officers dead and no arrests. An anonymous phone call informed the officer in charge of the investigation that the bodies in the burnt-out house in Redhill were those of Billy Mays and his men, and accused them of the murders. It looks like the truth will never be known."

"Maybe not, but perhaps they did kill them. You said yourself that since those bodies in the house were discovered no one has seen Mays or his men."

"True. If they are dead, I wonder who killed them. You were very interested in Billy at one stage."

"Yes, but that was because he was trying to kill my friend, Alan."

They carried on talking until the pub closed. Mickey could not rid himself of the nagging feeling that somehow Ransome was involved in Mays' disappearance; not that it bothered him very much, it was good riddance as far as he was concerned.

Late in November, Alan and Lynne got married, and Ransome was best man. At the reception, Lynne and Akira were chatting.

"You looked radiant in that white wedding dress."

"Yes, it did look good, didn't it? None of it would have been possible if John hadn't brought us together again. I'm hoping Alan makes me pregnant; we both want kids."

"So do John and I, but we haven't been lucky so far; we have to go for some tests."

"Are you thinking of getting married?"

"I would like to," Akira said smiling. "I'm twisting John's arm, and I think he will give in soon."

They both glanced at Ransome and Alan talking in a corner of the room.

"Without your help, John, this wedding would not have been possible," Alan said.

"You saved my life. Billy and his killers had to go down."

"Has Akira pressed you to get married?"

"Yes, but no date has been set. What are you going to do after the honeymoon?"

"I'm going to work as a bodyguard for a while. Are you going to stay in the police?" "Yes, but only for a short time. I want to leave the force and start my own firm specialising in criminal investigation and security. I was hoping you might join me; we made a good team in the Legion."

"When you're ready, John, I'll be glad to."

PIRATES

Four months later, Ransome left the police and rented a small office in Haringey. The firm was called John Ransome Investigations and Security. Alan joined him shortly after. Ransome had friends and contacts in the police and the Legion. At first, the work came in slowly, but gradually, it began to pick up.

One morning, Ransome phoned Stellman in New York.

"John, you must be psychic, I was about to ring you. I was speaking to the Emir of Qatar an hour ago. One of his tankers, the Noble Sword, has been seized by pirates. It was carrying two million barrels of crude oil worth $100 million. The pirates want $25 million for its safe return. Of course, he could pay the money, but he thinks it's time the pirates were taught a lesson. He wants some mercenaries to get his tanker back and I mentioned your name; do you think you could organise a force to do this?"

"Yes."

"Good. I will let him know and someone will get in touch with you in a day or two. I hope you pull it off."

When Alan returned to the office with a couple of coffees, Ransome told him about his call to Stellman.

"This job's big, John. Do you think we can do it?"

"Yes. We need something like this. It would put us on the map; if we succeed, word would get around."

"How many men are we going to need?" asked Alan.

"I think eighteen will be enough for this mission, so we have to find another sixteen. What I want you to do is phone your friends in the SAS and the Special Boat Service, and see how many men you can get for the job. They have to be available at short notice; tell them it's a one-off job but give no details. We cannot make a move until we hear from the Emir's representative."

The next morning, Ransome was sitting in his office drinking a coffee when the phone rang.

"Mr Ransome? My name is Faisal Al-halid. I believe you talked to Mr Stellman yesterday. Perhaps you can come and see me today at 12.30 p.m. I'm staying in the Mayfair Suite at the London Hilton."

"I'll be there."

Ransome went to the Hilton and knocked on the door of Al-halid's suite. It was opened by one of his bodyguards, who led him into reception. Faisal Al-halid greeted him with a handshake and a smile. He was about forty, tall and slim with short black hair and a thick moustache. They sat down, and he looked at Ransome with dark, suspicious eyes.

"We've checked you out, Mr Ransome; do you think you can recapture our tanker?"

"Yes, it's possible."

"How would you do this?"

"I think a force of eighteen ex-Special Forces operatives could accomplish it. We would drop into the sea at night near the tanker and launch our attack."

"Apart from money, what would you need from us?"

"A detailed plan of the tanker, its exact location on the night of the attack and equipment to navigate to it. We need arms and Zodiac dinghies, a plane to drop us and our equipment. After we are in control of the tanker, we need to be picked up by unmarked helicopters."

"And how much would this cost us, Mr Ransome?"

After some haggling, a sum of £3,000,000 in cash was agreed upon; half to be picked up two days before they left, the rest after the job was done.

"How soon can you do it?"

"In about fourteen days."

"Now, make me a list of what you need and I will contact you when we have all your supplies. Phone me when you and your men are ready to go. You can pick up £1,500,000 here, two days before your departure."

Ransome returned to his office and spoke to Alan.

"It's on. How many men were you able to get?"

"Six from the SAS and eight from the SBS."

"Good; see if you can get two of our friends from the Legion. The job is worth £3,000,000; we pay the men £50,000 each, £25,000 before they go and the rest when they return. We take £1,000,000 each, and the £200,000 we put into the business. How does that sound?" Alan smiled. "I like it; £1,000,000 is good pay."

A week later, Ransome's Army, as Alan called them, met for a briefing in a meeting room.

"You are, no doubt, keen to know what our mission is. It is to rescue the twenty-five-man crew of a Qatari oil tanker called the Noble Sword and return control of it to its owners. It was captured by Somali pirates southeast of Mombasa, Kenya. It was fully loaded, so it was probably not that hard to board, and it is now anchored off Ely on Somalia's northeastern coast. The pirates operate by using high-powered speedboats, launching their attack by firing automatic weapons and rocket-propelled grenades. They board the ships with grappling hooks and ladders. We shall fly from a Qatari airport and be dropped off near the tanker with our supplies. We shall navigate to the ship in four Zodiac dinghies. Once there, we shall climb both sides of the vessel and shoot dead any pirates we encounter.

"We leave for Qatar on Sunday. Come back here on Friday evening for your first payment of £25,000. This mission is top secret and must come as a complete surprise. Tell no one. Now, any questions? No? Good. Let's go down to the pub for a drink!"

On Friday, Ransome and Alan went to see Faisal Al-halid at the Hilton to pick up the £1,500,000, talk about the rescue of the hostages and to get the latest information on the tanker. On Sunday, they all flew to Qatar, arriving six hours and forty-five minutes later at Doha International Airport. After a short fifteen-minute ride, they booked into their hotel.

The next morning, Ransome and Alan went to check their supplies.

"Everything is here, Alan: the guns, the sniper rifles

and the Zodiac dinghies. They have done a good job. Now, let's go and see Faisal Al-halid in his office."

He told them that the exact location of the tanker was now known and they discussed the final details of the attack. When they got back to the hotel, Ransome gave his men a final briefing.

The next day, they left Qatar in a Qatari transport plane. Once they were over the jump zone, their supplies and Zodiac dinghies were pushed out and they jumped into the night. The sea was calm as they swam towards the flashing lights of their Zodiacs; it was 2.00 a.m. After retrieving their supplies and loading them into the dinghies, they used their tracking equipment to navigate towards the Noble Sword. Upon reaching it, they split up into two teams of nine: one was headed by Ransome, the other by Alan. They were dressed in black, and had night vision goggles and throat mikes. Two of them were armed with FN 30-11 sniper rifles, the rest with HKMP7A1 submachine guns fitted with silencers and extended 40-round magazines; some also had rocket-propelled grenades. They boarded the tanker using grappling hooks and ladders. Ransome's team reached the top deck first, followed closely by Alan's. They moved fast, killing six pirates on the way. Alan went down to the cabins to rescue the crew while Ransome's team went forward to take the bridge.

About three hundred yards before they reached it, Ransome stopped his men and said to his two snipers, "Shoot the pirates on the bridge."

After they stopped firing, they charged the bridge. Inside, they found three bodies.

Ransome said to his snipers Tom and Kirk, "That was good shooting; stay here and guard the bridge. We're going down to the cabins."

Meanwhile, Alan was leading his team down to the cabins next to him was Dillon, an ex-SAS trooper. As they entered the corridor where the crew was being held, they spotted two guards. They opened fire and cut them to pieces. Their pockets were searched and a bunch of keys was found. There were twenty cabins: the first four were unlocked and empty, and the fifth one was locked. As they were about to unlock it, another cabin door opened and an unarmed pirate stepped out. He saw the armed men in the corridor and yelled, then rushed back into his cabin to get his Kalashnikov rifle. The other three pirates woke up. Alan threw a grenade into their cabin and killed them all. The noise alerted the other pirates; they poured into the passage and a fierce fire fight ensued.

It was at this point that Ransome and his men arrived. As the pirate losses mounted they retreated, and were hunted down and shot. After the whole ship had been cleared and the crew was safe, Ransome used a satellite phone to inform Faisal Al-halid that the tanker was taken and the crew was safe. Later, he talked to his men.

"We've done well. The tanker is secure, the crew is safe, the pirates have been wiped out and none of us have been killed; although four of us have been wounded. The tanker was a big prize for them and there is a chance that more pirates may come and try to recapture it, but we will fight them off. Now the prisoners we have are friends or relatives of the dead pirates, get them to help you throw the bodies overboard. Then we will let them leave in two boats. The shore is not too faraway. When the tanker is in safe waters, we shall be taken off by helicopters."

After his speech, Ransome and Alan went to the bridge, where they spoke to the captain.

"I haven't thanked you properly for our rescue. Who are you?"

"Our identity must remain a secret. You know, Captain, more of them may come; if they do, we will be ready for them."

After spending some time talking to him, they returned to their men. Ransome spoke to Colin, an ex-SBS trooper and a friend of Alan.

"Have all the pirates killed on the top deck been thrown off?"

"Yeah, they're swimming with the fishes. There are about ten more bodies to be brought up from the lower deck."

Ransome and Alan returned to the bridge and spent some more time talking to the captain and looking through powerful binoculars.

Some time later, the prisoners were released and the Noble Sword sailed away. It was in the afternoon when they came in six speedboats. Alan saw them first. Tom and Kirk, the two snipers, started firing at the first boat, killing the helmsman and his companions. As the other boats came closer, they were hit by the concentrated fire of their HKMP7A1 submachine guns and more fire from the snipers and rocket-propelled grenades. They kept firing until all the pirates were dead.

After the attack was over, Ransome spoke to the captain.

"I do not think they will return again. We will stay with you until the tanker reaches safer waters."

They were picked up by unmarked helicopters two days later. The daring rescue made headline news across the world, and reporters questioned the crew who told them that after they were set free, their rescuers would not answer any questions and kept to themselves. They were unable to see the Emir, and all his spokesman would say was, "No comment." But reporters aren't stupid and thought that they were mercenaries hired by the Emir.

Back in London, Ransome and Alan collected the rest of the money and were congratulated by Faisal Al-halid and Stellman on their successful mission. They kept their business accommodation for a while; after all, a dingy office in Haringey was unlikely to be the headquarters of a firm sending mercenaries abroad. Their identities were unknown to the general public, but others knew, as did MI6 and the CIA.

Akira was relieved to have him back again. When he had gone away he gave no details, but said it was a big job. Now that he had more money, they moved into a large flat in Richmond.

A month later, Ransome and Alan were discussing business.

"You know, Alan, we've got good jobs coming in, and it's time we moved to larger premises."

“True, you were right about that job putting us on the map. Have you got anywhere in mind?”

“Yes, I’m going to Liverpool Street to look at some offices this afternoon, and I want you to come with me.”

They liked the offices they were shown and arranged to move in at the end of the following month.

THE RECEPTIONIST THROWS KNIVES

Back in their office, Ransome decided to phone an employment agency for a receptionist. Over the next few days he interviewed four women, but he didn't like the look of any of them. He wanted someone reasonably good looking, alert and friendly. The fifth woman who came in seemed to be more what he was looking for, and he asked her to sit down.

"What's your name?"

"Donna Hammerson."

He looked at her. She was in her mid- twenties, an attractive brunette with green eyes. As they talked she seemed friendly enough, but there was some sadness in her eyes.

"Can I see your CV?"

As he was looking at it, she thought about Jimmy and how they had met. It was on a Saturday afternoon in early spring. She had been paid the previous day and had gone up the West End to buy a new dress. She had found what she was looking for and was pleased with her purchase. As she walked along, she noticed a tall, good-looking guy coming towards her – he wore black trousers and shoes, a white shirt and a grey jacket.

He stopped in front of her and said, “Donna, is that you?”

She looked at him in puzzlement. She thought, *‘He’s handsome, but who the hell is he?’*

“I’m Jimmy, don’t you recognise me? We were in the same class.”

She looked at him closely. “You look a bit like him, but he was so skinny a puff of wind would have blown him away.”

“Yeah, but I got into bodybuilding and lifting weights.”

They were looking at each other and liked what they saw.

“Let’s go, I want to buy you a drink.”

“Okay.”

They found a pub and he ordered the drinks. After they were sitting comfortably, they started talking.

“So what have you been doing since you left school?” he asked her.

“Office work mainly. I work as a receptionist, and you?”

“Oh, I knocked around a bit from job to job. I’m now Franco the Knife Thrower.”

Donna looked at him and burst out laughing, until there were tears in her eyes. “You’ve got to be kidding, Jimmy?”

“No, it’s true.”

“And how did you become a knife thrower?”

“I was working in London and was bored with my job. I had some money saved and decided to go to America for a holiday. I travelled around, and one day I was in Cincinnati when the circus came to town. I watched one of the shows and later went for a drink in one of the bars. A guy came in and we started talking and drinking. I recognised him as the knife thrower; he said he was retiring soon. He asked me what I was doing and I said nothing in particular, so he said, 'Why don't you join the circus? I will teach you to throw knives and in a couple of years you will have my job.' The idea was crazy, but I did just that, and after two years Frank retired and I became Franco. I had a partner called Jessica, and we were the knife-throwing act 'Franco and Jessica', but she left later to get married. Now I'm looking for a new partner."

Donna looked at him and said, "Do you expect me to believe all that, Jimmy?"

He didn't say anything, but suddenly a knife appeared in his hand. He got up and walked over to the dartboard, took aim and threw the knife. It was a bull's-eye.

He said to the barman, "Just trying to impress the girlfriend."

"I'm not your girlfriend."

"You soon will be. Come on, let's go. Now do you believe me?"

"Yeah, I guess so."

They soon became lovers. She left her job and went to America with him, and became his partner in the knife-throwing act. When he was killed in a traffic accident, she took it very badly and decided to return to London and get a job so she would have something new to focus on.

Ransome interrupted her thoughts. "I see from your

CV that you haven't worked in London for three years; where were you during that time?"

"In America working with my boyfriend, until he was killed in a traffic accident."

"I'm sorry to hear that. What kind of work were you doing?"

"We were a knife-throwing act."

Ransome looked at her in amazement. "Really?"

"Yes."

"And did he teach you to throw knives?"

"Yes, he did. His real name was Jimmy, and he also liked guns and would go to firing ranges. I got fed up with staying at home and began to go with him. I can throw knives; it helps me to relax and I practise every week. I enjoy shooting guns as well, and can use various pistols and submachine guns."

Ransome smiled. A woman with aggressive talents! "If your references are okay, you can have the job. It starts at the end of next month. I will ring you in a few days."

He checked her references over the next few days and, finding them satisfactory, she was soon working at their new offices in Liverpool Street.

One evening, as they were leaving work, Ransome said to Alan, "Donna, our new employee, is not only a receptionist but also throws knives and fires pistols and submachine guns."

Alan smiled. "John, you need a holiday; you're losing your mind."

"No, it's true, I've checked her out; she was in a knife-throwing act, but her partner, who was also her boyfriend, was killed in a traffic accident. She used to go with him to gun ranges. We may be able to use her on one of our jobs. She's quick on the uptake."

A week later, he spoke to her in reception. "You've met Alan, haven't you?"

"Yes."

"Well, he's now working undercover in a drug company. Information about a new drug they are developing is being leaked to a competitor, and he is trying to find out who is responsible. He's got a few suspects and needs a woman working undercover to help him draw them out; men sometimes have a looser tongue when attractive women are around. I have told him about your background and we both think you are suited for the job – the pay will be better. I'll come back in an hour to give you time to think it over."

When he returned, she gave him her answer. "Yes, I would like this assignment. It will be very different from what I've done before."

"Good. You will be posing as an employee in the human resources department. Alan will give you the details."

It took four weeks before Alan was able to catch the member of staff who was selling the secret documents. Afterwards, Alan and Donna went to an expensive restaurant to celebrate.

"You know, Donna, you were a great help to me, and without you I don't think I would have been able to catch the guy who was passing on the secrets. You've done a good job; you don't have to return to the reception, we have other jobs we can offer you."

"Yes, I like this sort of work."

The next day, when Donna returned to the office, there was a new receptionist sitting behind the desk. She knocked on Ransome's door and went in.

"Ah, Donna, nice to see you again. Take a seat. You did a good job helping Alan. Did you like working undercover?"

"Yes."

Ransome smiled. "I think you're a bit adventurous and, like me, not a nine-to-five type. I would like you to go on a Close Protection course. We will pay for it of course. Some of our clients prefer female bodyguards. Would you be interested?"

"Yes," she said.

"The course is in three days' time."

After he had given her the details, she went home, had a drink and a piece of chocolate cake and thought about the job. It was supposed to be receptionist work but had turned into something else; life was now pushing her in a different direction. The pain of Jimmy's death was easing, but he was always there.

Donna passed the Close Protection course and worked as a bodyguard. She did more undercover work and became a valuable member of Ransome's team.

SHOOTING AT A CAR PARK

It was hot and getting hotter that Saturday afternoon in early June, Ransome and Akira were on their way to see her parents. They had become thirsty, so they stopped their car at a large pub near Brighton called the Pig and Whistle. They went in and bought drinks at the bar, then went over to some seats in the corner. As they sat there talking and drinking, two men came in, bought their drinks and sat at the bar looking around. They were the Gomez twins Lino and Carlos, Columbian gangsters – smartly dressed, strong, muscular and broad shouldered. They thought they were attractive to women, but the truth was they were rather ugly, and the only women who tolerated them were whores. Years of breaking the law and getting away with it had made them arrogant and nasty.

Lino saw Akira and Ransome sitting at a corner table and said to his brother, "Look at that Chinese girl sitting at that corner table with that guy; she looks good, I want her."

Akira noticed them looking and said, "Do you know those two men sitting at the bar, because they keep staring at us?"

"No, I've never seen them before."

Ransome stared at them and they looked away. Just then his mobile rang.

"Yes, it's me. Can you hold on a few minutes? I'll move where it's a bit quieter. To Akira, he said, "I'm going outside for a while, it's one of my clients."

As he was leaving the pub, he had a good look at the two men who had been staring at them. After Ransome left, Lino said to his brother, "Let's go over to her; he's gone."

They walked over to her table and sat down. Akira looked at them with barely concealed contempt. Lino put his hand on her knee and said, "Come with us, we can have a lot of fun, and we pay well."

"Take your hand off my knee, my boyfriend is outside."

"That doesn't worry us."

She tried to push his hand away, but he was strong. She got very angry and threw the remainder of her drink in his face. Lino was furious; no woman had ever dared to treat him that way before. He was so mad that he was about to draw his gun and kill her when Carlos quickly whispered in his ear, "Not here, we'll do it outside."

They got up and left. After they had gone, Akira wanted to tell Ransome what had happened so she got up and left the pub. They were waiting for her; she never stood a chance, as they shot her at close range. Ransome had seen her being killed and rushed in to attack them, but as he came closer they shot him in the shoulder and beat him up, then drove away in their car. Afterwards, the police were called. Akira's body was taken away and

Ransome went to the hospital. The bullets were removed from his shoulder and he was put in a private room. His parents came to see him; his mother was happy that he was still alive but very upset at what had happened. Alan and Lynne also came to visit. Alan ran the business in his absence. Ransome was questioned by the police and he described the killers and what had happened; a murder inquiry was started. The fact that he was a former police officer meant he was treated differently than if he had been an ordinary member of the public. The police had looked at the CCTV footage taken from the pub and had Ransome's description. They made enquiries and identified the men as the Gomez twins, and circulated their pictures.

On the fifth day of Ransome's recovery, Mickey came to see him.

"How you feeling, John?"

"Bullets slow me down."

Mickey smiled and said, "Not much else does." Mickey was now in charge of the Drug Squad.

Ransome asked, "What can you tell me about the Gomez twins?"

"There is an older brother, Eduardo, they all speak English and smuggle a lot of cocaine to the US, their main market. Last year, Lino was charged with rape and murder, and Carlos was also charged with murder, but they were both released after the witnesses disappeared. They think they're above the law. They sell drugs to Ron Spencer, who smuggles them into the UK. They like it here and come twice a year. I don't think they're going to be caught, and I would not be surprised if they return next year. I'll keep you informed if I receive any fresh information."

After he left, Ransome lay on his bed thinking. He was going to kill them; it was just a question of when and where. He would wait to see if they came back to Britain; if they didn't, he would go to Colombia and kill them there.

When he recovered, he left the hospital, and shortly afterwards Akira's funeral took place. Her family attended, as did his. He spoke to Akira's parents.

"I loved her, now she's dead and her killers have escaped, but I promise you, justice will be done, their time will come."

When the funeral was over, he went back to his flat where they had lived. Staying there brought back too many memories of their life together, and he was finding it very hard to get over her death. They had planned to get married in August. He decided to go back to work. Mickey had been right: the twins got away and returned to Colombia to carry on with their drug trafficking.

THE TWINS RETURN

Ransome and Mickey went for drinks sometimes, but it was not until six months later that he heard some important news about the twins. He was in his office one day when he got a call from Mickey.

"John, let's have a chat tonight at eight o'clock. Meet me at the usual place."

Ransome arrived at the pub first, and just as he was about to order a drink Mickey arrived and said.

"let's talk in my car."

Once they were sitting in his car, Mickey said, "The twins are back. One of my snouts was having a drink in a club in Berkeley Square when they walked in with two expensive looking whores. He recognised them because their pictures had been in the papers and on the TV. They had grown moustaches, but he was certain it was them. He got as close to them as possible. They were drinking and talking to the women, and in-between they were speaking to each other in Spanish. They sell drugs to Ron Spencer. We've been trying to catch him with a shipment of drugs for a long time, but without success, so we bugged his phones and during one call he mentioned that

L and C are coming soon. It's all beginning to tie in now. Now, this is not the end of the story. My snout followed their car after they left the club; they were careless and didn't notice, or maybe they were thinking about the pounding they were going to give those two whores. Anyway, they ended up in a secluded house in Leatherhead – I've got the address. You have two options. The first is to let us handle this and arrest them for murder; there is enough evidence to convict them, but you know what will happen: they will serve a few years in jail, and then they will be deported back to Columbia, free to carry on with their life of crime. There's no real justice in this country but plenty of do-gooders who think that a few years in jail is adequate punishment for murder. All murderers should be executed. The second option is you pay them a visit. I think you deserve your revenge." He handed him the address.

Ransome got out of the car and went back to his flat.

The next day, he left work at the usual time. He went home and got ready for his visit to the twins' house in Leatherhead. He got out a holdall and put his favourite weapons inside: an HKMP7A1 silenced submachine gun with three extended 40-round magazines and a Glock 17 pistol. He arrived at the house just after 9.00 p.m. and left his car some distance away. He climbed over the wall into the front garden and went round to the back of the house. He got in through the bedroom window on the ground floor, then opened the bedroom door and went into the passage. As he walked along he heard a noise coming from one of the rooms. He pushed the door open and went in. Fernando, one of the twins' men, was watching television with the volume set very high. When he saw Ransome he went for his gun, but he wasn't quick enough and Ransome cut him down with a long burst from his HKMP7A1. Then he searched the whole house, after which he hid Fernando's body and sat down to wait for the twins.

Hours later, he heard a car approaching on the gravelled driveway. He got up and waited out of sight near the front door. Lino came in first, carrying a large suitcase. When he saw Ransome, he was struck with fear as the bullets ripped through his chest. He was dead before he hit the floor. Carlos had entered just after his brother, but the shock of seeing his brother killed paralysed him for a few moments as Ransome pulled the trigger and shot him dead. He looked down at the bodies and hoped the twins would soon be reunited in hell. He wondered what was in the suitcases they had been carrying. They were both full of fifty-pound notes, probably from Ron Spencer for drugs he had bought from them. He spent some time in the house removing any evidence that might incriminate him, and when he was satisfied he left with the two suitcases. When he returned to his flat, he counted the money. Each suitcase contained £1,000,000.

The next day, he phoned Mickey.

"Let's meet tonight, usual place at 9.00 p.m."

"Okay."

Mickey saw him coming with a suitcase and got out of his car.

"You going on holiday, John?"

"No, I need to put this in your boot."

Mickey smiled. "What is it, John, a fucking bomb?"

"Yeah, you never did pay for the last round of drinks."

After the suitcase was put away and the boot locked, they got in the car.

"It's done, Mickey. They are dead and so is one of their men." He went on to describe what had happened at the house. "I also found some money there; must have been a payment from Ron Spencer for drugs he had bought from them. I've removed all the evidence that could incriminate me and got rid of the HKMP7A1. That suitcase in your boot contains £500,000."

"Bloody hell, John ... thanks."

EDUARDO

Two days later, Ransome was reading the evening paper in his office. The headline read *Three Men Shot Dead in Leatherhead*. He carried on reading about police acting on a tip-off and going to a house in Leatherhead, where they found the bodies of three unidentified men riddled with bullets. He put the paper down and called Alan.

He read him the article and then said, "I've killed the twins; the third man was one of theirs. Justice has been done, but there is going to be a problem. There is a third brother, Eduardo, and he's not going to take their deaths lightly; he's going to want revenge. From what I've learnt, he heads a very rich and powerful organisation, and I'm sure when he finds out that I've killed them, and I think he will find out, he will send his killers to London. We will have to be very vigilant."

"I'm glad you've avenged Akira's death, John. Those men deserved to die."

The next day, there was another article about the shootings, naming the dead men.

Ransome was right – Eduardo was not taking his

brothers' deaths lightly; in fact, he flew into a rage. His men had never seen in him in such a temper.

"Those fucking gringos, I'll kill them with my bare hands, beat them to a pulp and cut them into little pieces."

It took some time for him to calm down. Once he had, he sent for Luis Perez, a lawyer who represented his men when they were arrested. Perez was a man who loved money and the good life, even if it meant working for gangsters.

"Luis, my brothers were killed in London. I'm not sure exactly who done it. You're smart and speak good English, and I want you to go to London to find out who killed them. The way I see it, it could have been Ron Spencer, a man I do business with, or maybe it was the boyfriend of the woman they were accused of killing; although it would have taken a lot of balls to face them. I don't know anything about him, so find out. Or it might not have been either of those two but someone else. I must have the identity of whoever killed them. Take this package – there is $30,000 inside. When you come back with your report and I am satisfied, I will give you another $50,000. I want you to phone me regularly with your progress; also, I want you to rent a house in London and bring me back the keys."

After Luis left the house, he booked a flight to London. While on the plane he gave careful thought to how he would handle the assignment, and when he arrived in London he went straight to his hotel and phoned Ron Spencer's number, but got no reply. He was tired and decided to call it a day.

The next day, he went to the house. The door was opened by an attractive brunette of about thirty.

"Yes, can I help you?"

"I'm Luis Perez. I work for Eduardo Gomez. I need to speak to Mr Spencer."

"Come in, I'm his wife." She knew Ron bought drugs from Gomez and smuggled them into the UK. It didn't bother her that he sold drugs; the living was good, her wardrobe was full of expensive dresses and shoes, and there were always exotic holidays. What really bothered her was Ron's heart attack. She didn't want her lifestyle to end.

She led Perez into the lounge and asked him to sit down.

"I have to see your husband; where is he?"

"In hospital, he's had a heart attack."

"When did that happen?"

"On the fourth of December at 11 p.m."

"Can you phone him? I must see him."

She made the call, and he went to Spencer's private room at the hospital. They shook hands, and he sat down near his bed.

"Mr Perez."

"Call me, Luis."

"I think the only reason you have come here is to find out if I or my men killed the twins. The plain answer is no. I've been doing business with Eduardo for over two years, and I have always paid in full and on time. I didn't know where they were staying and had no reason to kill them. I know better than to cross Eduardo. I will tell you what happened," Spencer said. "They arrived after

8.00p.m. and I gave them two suitcases, each containing one million pounds. After they left at 9.00 p.m., I played cards with my men until I had a heart attack at 11.00 p.m. I was taken to hospital, and my men went as well."

Luis had spent years dealing with criminals. He knew when they were lying, and he thought Spencer was telling the truth. Luis checked the time Spencer had arrived at the hospital – 11.32 p.m. He also checked if his men had come with him – they had. He drove back to Spencer's house and then to Leatherhead. It took him over five hours. The twins had been killed at 2.00 a.m. There was only one way that Spencer's men could have killed the twins at that time, and that would have been if they had followed their car; though he didn't think that could have happened because the twins would have spotted them.

The next day, he went out and checked old newspapers that showed details of Akira's murder. He read that her killers were Colombian gangsters called the Gomez Twins. After they shot her dead, her boyfriend went to to grapple with them. They shot him in the shoulder and beat him up, then drove off in their car. The boyfriend's name was John Ransome. The incident happened outside a pub near Brighton called the Pig and Whistle. There was a warrant issued for their arrest, but they had escaped back to Colombia. Luis didn't really understand why the woman was killed and found it strange that Ransome never spoke to the newspapers or other media about the crime. He had to learn more about him and so decided to hire a private detective.

He found one near King's Cross and went up to his

office on the second floor. The nameplate on the door read *Brent Investigations*. He knocked on the door and went in; sitting behind a desk was Jake Copsmith, a large man in his early forties. He was reading a newspaper.

"Mr Copsmith?"

"Yes."

"My name is Perez."

"Take a seat, Mr Perez. What can I do for you?"

"I need you to get all the information you can on a man called John Ransome. It's a private matter."

"I'm sure it is, but I need some more information."

"My employer would like to give him some important information about a murder that he was investigating while a detective, which was never solved. He doesn't want to go to the police but wants to give it to Mr Ransome himself."

Copsmith wrote down the details and said, "If you give me your mobile number, I will ring you when I have the information."

What Luis didn't know was that Copsmith knew Ransome and, for a time, had worked with him in the police. Copsmith found his number and called him.

"Hello, John, it's Jake Copsmith."

"Hi, Jake, it's been a few years since I've seen you. How are you?"

"Not bad. I left the force and opened up a small firm called Brent Investigations. There's a Colombian lawyer enquiring about you, a man called Perez. He wants all the information I can get about you and he's given me a story that I think is complete bullshit. I think they want to find you and kill you."

"Thanks for calling me, Jake, I've been expecting something like this. You had better give him some information, otherwise he will go to somebody else. Tell him I've been in the police and have done five years in the Foreign Legion. Give him my home address and my business address."

"Are you sure about the addresses?"

"Yes, I will move out of my flat but will go to work as usual." He gave Copsmith some more details to pass on to Perez.

"John, be careful; these men are dangerous."

"Yes, I know."

After the call, Ransome phoned a letting agency and three days later moved into a flat in Victoria.

The next day, Copsmith called Perez. "I have the information," he said.

"Good, I will be there in an hour."

When he arrived, Copsmith handed him a small file on Ransome.

Luis read it and said, "I would have liked more details, but it will do." He paid Copsmith and left.

When he got back to his hotel he phoned Eduardo and booked a flight to Colombia.

When he arrived, he went to the house where Eduardo had been waiting impatiently. After exchanging greetings, Eduardo said, "Before you give me your report, have you rented the house?"

"Yes, here is the address and the keys. The information I got in London was that your brothers were killed on 5th December at 2.00 a.m. in Leatherhead, according to a police report. I went to see Ron Spencer; he had a heart attack at 11.00 p.m. the night before your brothers were killed and was taken to hospital – his men went with him. He told me your brothers arrived at his house after 8.00 p.m and he gave them two large suitcases, each containing £1,000,000 – payment for the last shipment of drugs. They left at 9.00 p.m. He said he didn't know where they were staying."

"Yes, I told them never to reveal their address," Eduardo interrupted. "It took me more than five hours to reach your brothers' house from Spencer's place. I don't think he had them killed. I usually know when people are lying and he didn't know the address, and even if he had found out, the killers couldn't have made it to the house by 2.00 a.m. unless they had followed their car, but I think the twins would have seen them. Now, this brings me to the dead woman's boyfriend, John Ransome; an interesting man, an adventurer and more than capable of killing your brothers. He killed a getaway driver and a bank robber when he was in the police Armed Response Unit; before that, he was in the French Foreign Legion, and he finished his service in the Elite Commando Unit. His motive would have been revenge; he was going to get married. I think he killed your brothers and took their money."

Eduardo asked more questions and told Perez that he had earned his $50,000. After he left, he called one of his men to come in.

"Benito, you're going to London. I'm sure I know who killed my brothers, an Englishman called John Ransome. Take three men with you – one of them has to be Jorge as he speaks English as well as you do. I do not want this man killed, I want him kidnapped and taken to a house we have in London. Here is the address and the keys. I wish to speak to him." He gave a cruel smile. "You leave in three days. Now go and make the preparations."

INCIDENT

After leaving Eduardo, Benito had a meeting with the three men: Jorge, Nino and Arturo.

"We're going to London," he said. "The man who killed Eduardo's brothers has been identified. He's a gringo called John Ransome. We're not going to kill him but kidnap him and hold him until Eduardo arrives." Benito smiled. "He would like to speak to him; the gringo will wish he had never been born."

When they arrived in London they took a cab to a house in Wandsworth Common. The next day, he showed them a picture of Ransome.

"Take a good look; this is the man we want. Jorge, you will be up early tomorrow, and for the rest of the week you will stand outside the building where his office is. Look as if you're on a break – smoke a cigarette occasionally. I must know his routine. Nino, you will steal two cars and change their number plates. On the day before the kidnapping, you will steal a van."

Ransome got up early that Monday morning. He opened the curtains and looked outside. It was cold, dark and raining heavily. He had spent part of the weekend lifting weights, jogging and practising his karate; he was in peak condition. After having a shower, he went into the kitchen and had a breakfast of steak and eggs followed by two coffees. His hunger satisfied, he went into the bedroom and started dressing. He liked to look smart and owned over twenty suits, as well as a large collection of shirts and ties. When he was ready, he looked the business. He went downstairs into the car park and got into his £230,000 184mph Bentley Brooklands and drove to pick up Alan. The car was expensive but business was good, and he had thought, *Hell, why not? I can afford it*.

As he was driving them to the office, they talked about the things they had to do that day, and just before seven o'clock they arrived outside the large office building In Liverpool Street. Ransome went to get a coffee while Alan parked the Bentley in the underground car park. On the way back to the office, he noticed a man smoking outside the building. He was about forty, foreign looking, a bit on the heavy side. He thought he was probably South American. He could feel his eyes on him as he walked past into the building. He didn't think much of it, but then he was there the next day and everyday, always watching him. He asked the security guard about him and was told that he didn't work in the building.

On Thursday evening, Benito gave his orders. "We will grab him tomorrow morning. Nino, you will be the driver. Jorge and Arturo will be waiting for him. After he has bought his coffee and walks past you, hit him on the head with the blackjack and throw him in the van. Then both of you will get in the van and stay with him until Nino drives you back to the house."

On Friday morning, Ransome saw that he was there with another man. They were standing near the open doors of a large van and there was a driver in the cab. As Ransome approached them, he threw his scalding hot coffee in Jorge's face, and he grabbed Arturo by the lapels and head-butted him. While Jorge cupped his scalded face in his hands, Ransome punched him in the stomach and then knocked him down. Arturo was groaning as he hit him again. Then, he threw both of them in the van and searched them. He put their pistols in his pockets, banged on the side of the van a couple of times and the driver sped away. Benito had been watching from the opposite side of the street and had seen that the kidnap had failed, but there was nothing he could do, so he got into the car and drove back to the house.

Ransome went back to get another coffee. Anna, who was behind the counter, said, "What? You've finished your coffee already?"

Ransome smiled. "Not exactly; someone else needed it more than me."

When Benito phoned Eduardo and told him that they had failed to kidnap Ransome, he was told to return to Colombia. When he arrived, Eduardo was with two men he didn't recognise.

"I'm very angry that you couldn't kidnap him. I wanted to put a bullet in his head myself. You're going back to London, and Dario and Juan are coming with you. Dario will be in charge; he's already killed forty men."

Benito could quite believe it. Dario was a sinister-looking man and everything about him was black, except his eyes: black hair, black moustache, black clothes. He was a man who could make people feel uncomfortable just by looking at them. Nino picked them up at the airport and took them to the house, where Benito introduced Dario and Juan. After they had all had some drinks, Dario spoke to them.

"Eduardo has put me in charge. In a few days, we are going to Ransome's office on the tenth floor to kill him and anyone else who is on that floor; it should not be difficult. Benito, Juan and Arturo will be coming with me. Nino will do the driving. Jorge, you will stay in the house. We will all be armed with Uzi submachine guns."

A week after the attempted kidnapping incident, Ransome and Alan were leaving the office and as they passed the reception desk, Josh Talbot, the security guard, said, "Can I have a word, Mr Ransome?"

"What's up, Josh?"

"After I left work last night, I was stopped in the street by a nasty-looking individual who asked me if I wanted to earn £500 and sell him some information about you and your company. He wanted to know how many people you employ, if you or your staff work weekends, and he also wanted to know about security in the building, When I refused to tell him anything, he got angry and walked away. He spoke English but with an accent I couldn't recognise."

"Thanks, Josh, I will speak to you about this again tomorrow."

Early the following morning, Ransome spoke to Josh.

“I’ve got a problem with some South Americans. I think they will be paying me a visit soon, so stay alert and press the red alarm button if you see any suspicious-looking characters going up to my floor.”

He gave him an envelope and took the lift to the tenth floor. After he left, Josh opened the envelope – there was £500 inside. Back in his office, Ransome was talking to Alan and Donna.

“I am convinced that these gangsters will be coming here soon. They will be armed and dangerous. I’m not going to run, that’s not my style, but it will be safer if you all stay away.”

Alan was the first to speak. “I’m not going, John. You will need help.”

Donna spoke next. “I’m staying too. I’ve been in some tough spots in my life, but I’ve always managed to get away somehow.”

Ransome looked at them in turn and said, “I could not wish for better friends. When all the staff are in, I’m going to tell them to work from home until further notice.”

DANGEROUS VISITORS

Juan was sitting in the coffee shop waiting for Ransome to show up. When Ransome came in and bought his coffee, Juan phoned Dario on his mobile and waited for him to arrive. Inside the stolen car making its way to Ransome's offices were Dario, Benito, Arturo and Nino. Dario spoke to Nino.

"Wait in the car for us; killing the gringos won't take more than fifteen to twenty minutes."

The Mercedes pulled up outside the coffee shop and Juan got in the back; then Nino drove away and stopped the car outside Ransome's building.

Inside the car, Arturo handed Juan an Uzi submachine gun and said, "Put that under your coat."

"You all know what to do," Dario said, "let's go."

They got out and walked through the entrance of the building. They didn't bother going up to the reception desk but went straight to the lifts. Josh had seen the four men come in. They had an evil look about them, and he knew instinctively that they were going up to Ransome's floor. He left the reception and went up to them.

"Excuse me, you are all visitors and will have to sign in."

Dario gave him an angry look and said, "Yeah, we'll do that when we come back."

Josh went back to the reception desk and pressed the red alarm button. As soon as they heard this on the tenth floor, Ransome, Alan and Donna got ready. Ransome waited near the reception behind the fire exit door, watching through the narrow glass panel in the door. Alan and Donna were in one of the offices.

As the lift was going up, the gangsters checked their Uzis. Dario said, "We must kill Ransome and anyone else who is there. It will be easy, they will be unarmed."

When they reached the tenth floor, the reception desk was deserted. Behind it were two offices, and on the right were another two offices and the fire exit door.

"Take care of the reception, then join us", Dario told Arturo. "We will be checking the rest of the floor."

Ransome had seen the lift doors open and moved out of sight. Arturo started checking the offices, while Dario and the others had turned left and through the double doors leading to the fifteen offices on the main floor. They split up and went individually to check each office. As Juan opened the door of one of the offices he was attacked by Donna, who sprayed his face with foam from a fire extinguisher, while Alan beat him with a baseball bat until he was unconscious. He then picked up his Uzi and said, "I'm going in the corridor, you stay here and get your knives ready."

The next time Ransome looked through the glass panel, he saw Arturo walking towards the double doors leading to the main floor. He had checked the offices but they were empty. He was disappointed; he wanted to kill someone. Ransome opened the fire exit door. Arturo heard the door open and looked back. It was only a short distance away, but he could not stop Ransome, who had moved swiftly and smashed him over the head with a 21-inch baton. He collapsed on the floor. Ransome picked up his Uzi and went through the double doors to the main floor. As Ransome walked along, Dario came out one of the offices. Ransome's reaction was fast, and he shot him dead before he could even aim his submachine gun. Just as he was picking up Dario's Uzi – as it had a full magazine – Benito suddenly appeared. He saw him from the corner of his eye and dived into the office from which Dario had come, Benito started firing into it.Alan saw him; opened fire with Juan's Uzi and killed him.

Ransome came out of the office. "Thanks, Alan. Some bullets just came too close."

When Dario and the others didn't return after twenty minutes, Nino phoned his mobile. Ransome picked it up and said in Spanish, "The party was a killer, nobody is coming back."

Nino didn't recognise the voice and realised something was wrong. He returned to the house and told Jorge, who called Eduardo in Colombia. He told him that they should both leave the house, book into a hotel and phone him. When they had found out what happened, Jorge phoned Eduardo back late at night.

"Dario and Benito are dead. Juan and Arturo are in hospital."

Eduardo lost his temper and shouted, "What the hell

are you doing there? He's just one man. Six of you can't handle a job like that? Both of you return to Colombia on the next plane."

KNIGHTSBRIDGE

The inquiry into the deaths on the tenth floor was conducted by Superintendent Larry Dent, a man whom Ransome had met when he was in the CID.

He was walking around with Ransome and said, "You had a busy morning in the office: two men shot dead, two unconscious." He paused to look at some bullet holes in a door and smiled. "Are your visitors always so friendly? Was your coffee that bad, John? You'll all have to come in for questioning."

They were taken away and interrogated separately. Dent questioned Ransome.

"Four armed men came to your offices. Did they come to rob you? Not likely; you do not keep any money there. So who did they come to kill? Donna, you or Alan? Not saying much, are you, John? Why would four Colombian killers come to your offices in London? And who sent them and a man to question the security guard about you and your staff? I suggest it was Eduardo Gomez. Your story about somebody you arrested when you were in the force wanting revenge is wearing a bit thin. Your girlfriend was murdered by the Gomez Twins who, despite a manhunt, were never captured and returned to Colombia. Six months later, they are back and found shot dead in Leatherhead." He stopped talking for a few minutes, then looked at Ransome and asked, "What do you know about that?"

Of course Ransome knew everything. He had killed them to avenge Akira and had taken their money – not that he was going to admit that, so he said, "I was questioned and my fingerprints were taken."

"Ah yes, fingerprints; the ones that were found in the house were of the Gomez Twins and one of their men. Somebody had done a good job of removing all other evidence."

The next morning, a statement was taken from Donna and she was released. Alan was questioned again, while Ransome was interrogated by Dent, who said, "All their fingerprints were sent to Colombia and they have been identified. Their leader, Dario Martinez, was a professional killer. The others worked for Eduardo Gomez, one of the biggest drug traffickers in Colombia. Although there is no evidence, I think that you killed the Gomez Twins to avenge Akira's murder and Gomez sent his killers in revenge."

Ransome was quiet for a couple of minutes and then said, "About the death of the Twins, I have nothing to say; as to what happened in our offices, Alan and I acted in self-defence against murderous thugs."

No charges were brought against Ransome or Alan and they were released. The attack in Ransome's offices made the headlines: *Gangsters Invade Liverpool Street Offices* and *Killers In The Office* were just two of them.

The news-hungry hounds of the press stuck their noses everywhere, but without much success. Donna refused to be interviewed, while Ransome and Alan dropped out of sight and couldn't be found. Ransome closed his firm and offices in Liverpool Street, and the business was reopened under a different name. Their clients were impressed by the way they had beaten off the attack.

In Colombia, Eduardo had left his house and gone to his office in Cali. He was talking to Miguel, one of his men.

"I must avenge the death of my brothers. The men I sent to London failed to kidnap him, and the attack on his offices was unsuccessful. He is a hard man to kill. The next attempt must succeed."

Shortly after they had moved into their new offices in Knightsbridge, Ransome spoke to Alan and Donna.

"Can you both come to my flat in Victoria tonight? I need to tell you something and I don't want to say anything in the office."

When they arrived, he gave them a drink and said, "Next week, I'm going back to my flat in Richmond; I don't need to stay here anymore The reason I asked you to come here is to talk about Eduardo as he is getting to be a problem; he keeps sending his killers to London. I'm getting a team together and going to Colombia to kill him."

"I'm coming too, John," Alan said.

"Good, I always feel better when you're watching my back. Donna, I want you to stay in London and look after the business."

Donna smiled and said, “I want to come too. I remember you saying I’m not the nine-to-five type, and you were right.”